COASTSIDE
DETECTIVES

COASTSIDE DETECTIVES

ARMANDO'S GOLD

MATTHEW F. O'MALLEY

authorHOUSE®

AuthorHouse™
1663 Liberty Drive
Bloomington, IN 47403
www.authorhouse.com
Phone: 1-800-839-8640

Published by AuthorHouse   10/26/2012

ISBN: 978-1-4772-8215-1 (sc)
ISBN: 978-1-4772-8214-4 (e)

WEEK I

T HE CLOSURE OF HIGHWAY One at Devil's Slide, the southern route out of Pacifica along the coast, was into its second week, bringing an added sense of quiet to this bucolic town just south of San Francisco. Coastal commuters who normally rush through Pacifica on their way to San Francisco were being forced to bypass the town and find an alternate means to the City, most opting to use Highway Ninety-Two, which added an hour or two to their travels.

The closure of Highway One due to a rockslide was no stranger to the residents along the coast, who had been dealing with this seasonal occurrence for years. It had been expected this year, as with every winter season: drenching rain displaced boulders from the sparsely vegetated Western slopes of Montara Mountain, with the ensuing pile of rock and soil clogging the highway. It always took several weeks for crews to shore up the cliff-hugging highway and to clear the debris from the roadway by dumping it into the Pacific Ocean below.

The expense of continually repairing the highway, added to the stress and costs to commuters and business owners, had resulted in a voter-approved plan to bypass this treacherous stretch of road by drilling a tunnel through Montara Mountain some years back. The completion of the Devil's Slide tunnel was still a year away from completion, so until then, Pacificans would continue to have the town to themselves during these seasonal commuter breaks.

And the longtime Pacifica residents that I bumped into seemed to revel in the added peace of less people rushing through their town. I'd never seen as many people smiling as when that highway closed. Sure, they grumbled about hiking trails in San Pedro County Park being closed, or the rock and mudslide scarring of Montara Mountain and the coastal mountain range that cradles Pacifica to the sea. And sure, they complained about their own personal minor backyard mudslides or street closures due to flooding, but I swear, all conversations ended with, "Isn't it nice to be able to get home so quickly without all the cars on the highway or shop in virtually vacant stores? Isn't it nice that it's so quiet?"

I always nodded in agreement. "Yes, yes, I like it quiet." But actually, I was getting quite tired of it. I was born and raised in San Francisco and I needed some action. The highway closure was getting on my nerves. It was too quiet without the commuters rushing home, clogging the highway, with the hum of their vehicles overpowering the sound of crashing waves. I missed the variety that transient faces and a rush of commuters bring to a place. I missed overhearing cell phone conversations from strangers as I went shopping, or seeing an unusual face as I ate dinner at Nick's or seeing the well-dressed businessman or businesswoman stopping in at The Grape in the Fog wine bar.

But mostly I was tired of the rain we were having. Rain, rain and more rain. It had been raining since winter began and we were now in March and that, too, was keeping this little town sleepy as people remained indoors, staying dry. Crime, background checks and infidelity had apparently all gone into hibernation, and this downtime was driving me nuts.

It seemed liked the only action to have that Wednesday morning was to take a soaking walk from my townhouse on Oddstad Boulevard to check the water level of San Pedro creek, and once there, that only told me something that I already knew: this was the worst winter I had experienced since moving to Pacifica. As San Pedro creek drained from San Pedro Country Park, running in and out of a culvert below Oddstad Boulevard, I watched as a brown, churning debris-filled maelstrom passed below me to make its way to the Pacific Ocean.

Eucalyptus, willow, leaves and branches all seemed to be jockeying for a position to stay above the deep and fast-moving current that would eventually drag them to the Pacific Ocean. Watching this play of nature made me ponder how steelhead ever survived traveling up this creek to spawn or make their way back to the ocean where the pounding surf must surely use the creek debris, along with their tiny bodies, to rework the beaches and cliffs. One of these days, I promised myself, I'd join one of the volunteer groups that helped maintain this park and find out how the steelhead survived this environment to become the little fry I first saw the previous summer. As soon as the clouds broke, I would march right into the ranger station and volunteer for a day or so . . . but right now wasn't the time, even if the ranger station was open. I was getting soaked and it was time to head to work.

It was late morning and I was at my desk at our office of Coastside Detectives in Pacifica's Linda Mar Shopping Center, just tooling around on the Internet when Joe Ballard, my business partner and friend, strode in, proud as a prize rooster, carrying in his hands the metal detector he had recently purchased from the Heartland America catalogue company. Joe was wearing a harsh-weather green fisherman's hat, a dark green REI rain resistant coat, and khaki cargo shorts that were wet around his thighs. On his feet he was wearing black Gator sandal shoes. His pale goose-bumped white legs reminded me of an uncooked chicken freshly pulled from refrigerator.

"Ain't you cold from the rain?" I asked, as I'd been trying to warm up and dry my own pants legs with a floor heater under my desk, my raincoat silently dripping water as it hung from the coat rack.

"You don't mind the rain when you're also getting hit by the ocean," Joe said as he hung his hat on the coat rack. "And as long as the top part is warm, the bottom half is fine."

I looked back at his Gators. "You do know you kill me every time I see you wearing those shoes. I consider them nothing less than the Honda Element of the shoe world. Ugly!"

"These?" Joe said, looking down at his shoes, "These are the best! Great for walking in the sand. Sort of like snow shoes with the wide front. All the holes let you shake the sand out of them."

Joe gently placed his metal detector against the fichus tree near our office front door, so that the round flat end of the gadget was cushioned in the dirt of the potted tree. He then gestured a 'stay put' move to the detector before standing tall at the front of our office, a grin on his face.

"All right," I said and gestured. "Out with it."

Joe was beaming, and then momentarily, he removed the non-lit Magnolia cigar that he kept affixed to the left side of his mouth and said, "Check out what I found."

He reached into his pocket, retrieved something small and flicked it with his thumb to me. I watched it as it twisted in the air and traveled halfway across the office. I caught it with both my hands, rubbed it and looked at it. It was a coin of some sort, thickly caked with sediment, but it was definitely a coin of some sort.

"Where'd you find this?" I asked.

"Out there," Joe motioned with his cigar. "Out there by the rocks on the South side of Pacifica beach. It's low tide so I thought with the storms and runoff, I'd check out that area before people started scouring the area for whatever washed up on shore. You know, with the storms we've been having, I expected that something good would get washed up, but I never thought I'd find something like this." Joe put his cigar back in his mouth and intently watched me as I handled the coin.

I could tell it was old, really old, but I still couldn't make out the markings on it; it was too crusty and only a fine layer of sediment would come off it with a flat rubbing of my thumb. The coin was thin and it was no longer a perfect circular coin, if it ever was one. Age, saltwater, and probably the rocks had taken their two cents out of it. I scraped at the crust with my thumbnail and finally reached the dull glitter of the coin's surface. Gold—it was a gold coin. My eyes bulged and I blurted, "I think you found gold, Joe!"

Joe's smile grew toothy and he slowly nodded. "And a piece of a legend."

"Hmm?" I said.

"I'll tell you what I think I found at the bar. Feel like a morning pick-me-up?"

I didn't immediately answer Joe. I was in my own little world, transfixed by the coin that was in my hand. "I think you're going have to take it somewhere," I said, "some restoration place, maybe a museum, where they'll be able to remove some of this caked-on sediment without harming it."

I turned the coin one last time in my hand then flicked it back to Joe, who caught it. He looked at it, holding it into the light and closing one eye as he squinted with the other and inspected it. "Feel like a drink?" Joe repeated.

"Sure," I said. "I could do with a warm up. Let's go."

I T WAS AROUND ELEVEN in the morning, brisk outside and twenty steps before we reached Cheers, the only bar in the Linda Mar Shopping Center. Cheers always has the shades drawn on the windows and the glass doors, leaving the place dark enough for lighthearted conversations.

"Heya Babe," Jill Faraway, the bartender, said to Joe as we walked in. "Hey Mike."

Both Joe and I greeted Jill with our warmest hellos.

"What'cha have?" Jill asked. "The usual?"

Both Joe and I nodded yes.

After Jill served us our drinks, Jill tilted her head toward the far end of the bar. I looked down and saw the only other customer in Cheers this morning. It was Arthur McCoy, our nefarious reporter from The Coastal Watch newspaper and author of such smash hit articles and editorials as "Why detective agencies are bad for small towns",

"More trouble at the beleaguered Coastside Detective Agency", and "Mike Mason—might be a Sea Slug."

I looked down the bar with contempt and I nudged Joe with my elbow. Arthur had seen us come in and had kept his head down once we settled down into our stools. He was now working on finishing his drink as fast as he could. He emptied his glass, grabbed his folded newspaper off the bar, adjusted his baseball cap low over his eyes to hide his face and attempted to give us a wide berth as he made his exit. I got up and stood to block his escape. Joe grabbed my arm to sit me back down, but I wasn't having any part of that; I put my arm out to stop Arthur in his tracks.

"Hey, good morning, Arthur," I said sarcastically warm, "what brought you to slither out of your hole so early in the morning?"

Not one to back down when confronted, Arthur tipped his hat back with his folded paper and made a solid stance. "Well hey, Mike. And Joe, so nice to see you!"

He was all cheesy smiles, "Hey Mike, haven't see you in awhile." Arthur pointed at me with the folded paper in his hand, "What'cha been up to? Peeped through any back windows lately? Hide in any especially skanky trash cans of late? Any good backroom shenanigans I should be aware of?"

I took a step toward Arthur and the newspaper bent against my chest. I was going to slug him. I really was. Not for anything he said this morning, but for so many things he had said or had written about me and Joe in the past. Joe sensed I was ready to go at it, so he grabbed my arm and pulled me back.

"Hey Joe," Arthur said, "why don't you give your boy here some lessons on manners?"

Joe leaned back in his stool, let go of my arm, looked at me, then at Arthur, and said, "I think he can handle himself."

"Sure. Sure," Arthur replied, "I heard how he has been able to take care of himself. Like any kid could with a pair of brass knuckles or a gun in his hands."

"Hey!" I said and I pushed Arthur in the chest with one stiff finger. "You're really getting too close to the line."

"Hey!" Arthur rolled his newspaper tight and pointed it at me like a stick. "You pushed me."

"I did nothing of the sort!" I said back. "But if you're not careful, you may just slip on some beer that you spilled and fall into me."

"He pushed me! He pushed me!" Arthur said again, looking for validation from Joe, who just shrugged with his hands as if to say 'what did you expect'. Arthur then looked at Jill, who responded with a quiet, "Sorry, I missed that."

Arthur looked back to Joe and decided to take a verbal swipe at him. "Hey Joe," Arthur said, "get clubbed by any old ladies as of late? I don't see you walking around with that cane anymore.'

Now Joe got up. A long and hard life may have taken some of the energy out of Joe, especially the past few years, with his bout with cancer and a beating fairly recently in the office by a smuggler, but he was no pushover and still ready for a mix-up. And although Arthur was still relatively young, spry and would put up a good fight, experience-wise, Joe would beat him, hands down.

Joe moved next to me so we stood side by side as we faced Arthur, and I got to hand it to Arthur, he didn't back down when confronted with two.

"Trying to get yourself another story, eh Art?" Joe said. "One where you are the star attraction."

I was ready. "Yeah, I'll give you a good story," I joined in. "One you'll never forget!" I clenched my hands and stepped toward Arthur, who finally cowered back.

"Boys, now boys!" Jill came to Arthur's defense. "No need to get violent in here. Take a seat. Here Art," Jill said, "I poured you another and you two, you sit back down."

Jill set Arthur's beer two vacant seats from where we had been sitting. "Come on," Joe calmly said as he took his old spot. "Take a seat." I followed Joe and sat in my place, taking a drink while Arthur grimaced, still tense from being prepared for a fight.

"I'm not sharing a drink with these two," Arthur finally said.

Joe took a drink, put his glass down, then looked to Arthur. "Look Arthur," Joe said, "you need to understand where our frustration is coming from." Joe sat straight up on his stool by pushing off his legs with both hands, "and I can see where you may have some animosity toward us for who we are, what we do. But maybe it is time that we called a truce. Made some sort of deal."

"A deal?" Arthur's faced changed as his interests was piqued. He was also obviously relieved that he wasn't going to be beaten to a pulp. "What kind of deal?"

"A deal?" I interrupted. "Why should we make a deal with him?"

"This better not be some kind of game you're trying to play," Arthur said.

"No game." Joe said. "I just want a bit of peace between us. Bring back some order and little bit of heaven to Pacifica."

"All right, I bite." Arthur said. "What kind of deal are you offering?"

"I'll give you a story," Joe said, "and you can direct your talents off us for some time."

"Depends on the story," Arthur smirked.

Joe dug into his pocket and fished out the coin he had showed me earlier and placed it on the bar. "Check this out." Joe said. He slid the coin down the bar to me. I looked at it again, and then kicked it with my index finger down to Arthur, who stopped it in mid-slide. "I came across it this morning." Joe said, "out on Pacifica Beach."

Arthur looked at the coin closely, turning it over in his hands, inspecting it. "Looks like gold," he said.

"That's what I think," Joe said. "Thinking maybe I found a bit of Armando's gold."

"Do you think?" Jill asked, joining Art in his inspection of the coin.

Joe grinned and nodded.

"All right you two, I can see you cooking up something. Out with it." Arthur motioned with his hand. "Who is this Armando?"

"Yeah out with it," I joined in. "I've been waiting to find out something about this coin."

"You never heard of Armando's Gold?" Joe asked.

"Can't say that I have," Arthur replied.

"Nope," I agreed.

"Ahh, I guess you're too young," Joe said to me. Joe unzipped his dark green REI raincoat to reveal an orange and green Tommy Bahama shirt I had given him some umpteen years ago. It was the brightest object in the bar. "You have to be of a certain age, when the tale was still circulating, and an old timer of Pacifica to remember it," Joe continued. "Probably no one outside of Pacifica really knows about it anymore and if it was written about in relation to San Francisco, Armando is probably just a footnote."

Arthur was working the coin in his hand, trying to get some of the sediment off of it. "Go on," he said, "I'm listening."

"Well, the story I remember," Joe continued, "is that Armando worked the land here during the time of Don Francisco Sanchez, the guy who pretty much was granted most of the land that makes up

Pacifica, back in the late eighteen-thirties by the then Mexican governor of California. Armando was an Ohlone, or what the Spanish originally called Coastanoan Indian. He lived and worked at Mission Dolores in San Francisco and somehow came to Don Sanchez's land and basically worked as a servant of some sort. Why he came back here, nobody really knows. Maybe coming back to ancestral lands, maybe to get away from Mission Dolores where so many of his people died. It's all speculation."

Joe took a swig of his drink to gather his thoughts and to see if we were paying attention. "Anyway," Joe continued, "in 1848 gold was discovered along the American river and Armando was swept up with the rest of the world and disappeared to the gold country. Sometime later he returned, with pockets and bags full of gold, nuggets and gold dust. Some say he went a little crazy. He lived big in San Francisco for a time, returning to Pacifica every so often to replenish his pockets from his stash. Word was he melted some of his gold down and pressed his own coins.

"What I remember," Jill interjected, "was basically that he became a drunkard in later life and died penniless."

"That's the official line," Joe said. "The legend goes something along the lines that on the last day he was seen, he was riding the train that used to run along down here and told one of the engineers that he had a great treasure hidden and that he would give it all to him. But then he never followed through. He just disappeared. Some say he was robbed by bandits. Back then, there were a bunch of bandits hiding out in the back areas of Pacifica. It was kinda sketchy back then. From then on, the tale just grew to say he had the money buried somewhere on the Sanchez Adobe land or in a cave somewhere up on Montara Mountain."

"I remember hearing that too." Jill said, "But I thought that was eventually proven to be incorrect and he just died broke."

"Again, that's the official line," Joe said. "There were a couple of instances where people got hurt, kids climbing around the mountain, searching for a cave where the gold was hidden, back in the seventies. After that, there was a campaign to put out 'the truth' that would squelch any more searches for caves or gold. You can probably find some records of it in your paper's archives." Joe directed his comment to Arthur.

Arthur had continued to work the coin with his thumb, rubbing it as Joe talked. "Hey," Art now said, "I think I can make out the outline of some sort of indentation!"

Jill bent over the bar to look closely at the coin in Arthur's hand. "Here, let me see it again," I said.

Arthur looked at me and I could see the anger that was once in his eyes had completely subsided and had been replaced with a tinge of excitement. He looked at the coin again then reached down the bar to place it in my outstretched hand. I looked at it again and passed it on to Joe.

"So if it is part of Armando's gold," Arthur asked, "how do you think you came across it, on the beach, from over a hundred years ago?"

"I was thinking about that," Joe said. "I was thinking that maybe all the shaking of the mountain they were doing building that new tunnel through Montara Mountain had shaken things up. Maybe some of the treasure has made it down to one of the creeks, washed some of the gold down out to the beaches."

"Maybe," Arthur replied. "But that wouldn't explain the crust around the coin. Seems like it's been in saltwater for quite awhile."

"Maybe it fell out of someone's pocket, or maybe someone tossed it into the ocean for good luck a hundred years ago and the recent storms just washed it ashore," Joe said. "I haven't figured that out yet."

"Or maybe," Arthur joined in on the speculation of the coin's discovery, "all the recent storms and low tides uncovered it. Just like the *Prince Phillip*, that 19th century cargo ship that ran aground out on San Francisco ocean beach back in the late 1870s. It recently was uncovered by the low tides and storms and is showing its skeleton after being buried by the sands for over a century."

"I don't think we'll ever know for certain with just this one coin." Joe sounded dejected. "We'd have to find a bunch more to start speculating."

"What are you planning to do with it?" Arthur asked.

"Well, that's what Mike and I were discussing a little earlier," Joe said. "Taking it to a museum or something."

"If I was you," Arthur suggested, "I'd think about taking it to the San Mateo County Museum, in the old courthouse in Redwood City. They have good people there."

Joe nodded. "Yeah, that's probably the best."

"Just one more thing," Arthur said, "if I may."

Joe shrugged with his hands to say 'just ask'.

"May I take a photo of it?"

"Sure." Joe nudged my arm with the back of his hand, so I passed the coin to Arthur. Arthur placed the coin on a white napkin on the bar, fished out a digital camera from his pocket, took several pictures, took out a quarter and placed it next to the coin, took a few more pictures, then flipped the gold coin over and repeated the process.

When Arthur had taken all the photos that he needed, he passed the coin back down and Joe placed it in his breast pocket.

"Good enough story?" Joe asked. "Truce?"

Arthur looked at both of us, then at Jill, who nodded in her agreement. "Good enough story." Arthur said as we all shook hands. "Truce."

As I took a slow last gulp of my Manhattan, I turned so I could look at Arthur through the bottom of my glass. His image was distorted and I watched him gathered himself and say his goodbyes to Jill before trotting off. So we now had a truce with Arthur McCoy, but it didn't mean I had to like him.

3

T HE WEEKEND WAS SPENT moving. Moving all the records, office furniture and supplies we had out in a storage unit on Palmetto Ave in Pacifica, to our new Tenderloin office. This Tenderloin office was actually our second foray into the area and indeed a throwback in time and place for us, as all the furniture and records that we were moving into this space were from the first detective office that Joe's father established in the Tenderloin back in the mid-1930s.

The move back to the Tenderloin was more Joe's idea than mine. I think with age, he's been growing nostalgic, though he professes it was more of a business decision for the long term viability of our company. He always says he follows his father's belief that you need two offices in the City, one in a good area, and one in a bad area. You knew you had a good case if someone who would normally be found in the Marina made their way out to the Tenderloin branch, not wanting to be recognized. For the location, we found a space across the street from the Tenderloin police station on Eddy Street. It gives a person a choice as to who they want to handle their current issues. It also gave us some solace, as hopefully our place would be less likely to be broken into, even with the barred windows and security gate. The smoked glass windows and smoked glass on the front door would also conceal the goings-on inside the office.

The office itself was cold and dark. The metal steam heaters, covered in peeling silver paint, clanked and spattered when they finally produced heat an hour after being turned on. The painted walls, having long suffered the days that allowed for indoor smoking, were a morose yellow and were peeling in many places. The bright spots in the place were the chandeliers that split the room down the center, and the beautiful crown molding. There were two rooms in the back office, one a lavatory containing old fixtures with a sink and toilet that produced orange-brown water in their bowls, and the other room being a small office. The rug throughout the place was a worn gray with little persimmon orange squares, while the bathroom had thick speckled linoleum. Throughout the space, the floors undulated like a wave stopped in motion.

Joe also backed the move to the Tenderloin, with the logic that he wanted to ensure this company would outlast him. Making Steve Parodi, our one time intern then computer wizard, a partner and manager of a revived Tenderloin office, was a step in that direction.

For his part, Steve was a little more than hesitant in accepting the offer. He was now twenty-six, a little introverted and not into confrontations, but he was more than ready to begin a full time career. He had another job when he first started interning then working with us, as a paralegal, but the hours, workload and little in terms of excitement, were not to his liking. What Joe offered him was thrills and intrigue, things he already had a taste of working with us, but now he would experience tenfold as he was to leave the safety and security of a desk and computer screen to confront real life issues.

For the move that weekend, it was Joe, Steve, Ozzie and me. Ozzie was our latest intern. We had him filling in twice a week, in the afternoons at the Marina branch, just to have a breathing body there. Joe had more ambitious plans for Ozzie as well, grooming him to be Steve's successor over there. Unlike Steve, who looked like Ichabod Crane at a buck-fifty, Ozzie was a little more on The Penguin looking side of things, nineteen years old, five-two and waddling at about two fifty with probably a pound of that as acne on his face alone. He said he was studying for a degree in criminology at SF State, but so far, I hadn't seen much in terms of motivation from the kid.

As soon as I pulled up to our new office and double parked the Uhaul, Steve and Ozzie having found parking around the corner, a routine assortment of well-wishers and an unlimited number of volunteers, your basic Tenderloin welcoming committee of criminals, druggies and indigents, showed up at the back of our truck, even with the police station just across the street.

Joe was the first to climb out of the Uhaul, randomly banging its side as he walked its length with a miniature souvenir Giants baseball bat. When he reached the back of the truck, he opened the door, climbed into the back and glowered down upon the gathered crowd. He adjusted his Magnolia in his mouth and glowered again. Some words were spoken but Joe got his point across and the denizens moved a respectable distance away, far enough to be out of Joe's reach but close enough that their drug-glazed eyes could still evaluate if there was anything thing of value being taken from the truck and brought into the office.

There wasn't much, though, to interest the most desperate. The furniture was all the original furniture Joe's father had brought in when he first opened up the business back in 1935: heavy oak desks and uncomfortable wooden chairs. Filing cabinets and boxes. Boxes upon boxes filled with old files. And just when we thought we were done carrying in all of the boxes, we found more boxes behind the last couple of cabinets we had in the truck.

It was when I was taking a break, talking to Joe as Steve and Ozzie manhandled the last filing cabinet through our office's front door, when I noticed someone making his way through the throng of onlookers. He was walking with a cane, a black fedora, and a black overcoat hanging off his shoulders that partially covered his white pin-striped suit, bright purple shirt and bright pink tie. He was looking at Joe, smiling with the biggest of smiles and looking as if he knew Joe.

"Hey Joe," he said when he reached the back of the truck. "Remember me?"

"Freddie?" Joe asked. "Freddie Jack?"

"Now I go by my full name," the man said, "Freddie Jackson."

Joe climbed down from the back of the Uhaul, took Freddie's outstretched hand and shook it. "Hey Mike, you know who this is?" Joe said excitedly, "It's Freddie! How you doing, Freddie?"

Freddie was a pimp we knew from back in the day. Indeed, Joe was the reason Freddie had his limp. Back then, Freddie knew us and we knew him and he did his best to avoid us when we were around after Joe gave him a piece of his mind and the limp. Now, time seemed to have softened both of their outlooks on each other.

Freddie tilted his head sideways and cocked an eye to try to get a flicker of remembrance and then said, "Oh yeah, I remember you." And that was all he said in reference to me.

"I thought you'd be dead by now," Joe continued, smiling as if they were old friends and again taking Freddie's attention. "Or in jail."

"Almost died several times," Freddie said, just as giddy. "And was in jail for a number of years. Heard the other day there was a new detective company opening up and I thought I'd drop by. Was wondering if you were moving back."

"Can't stay away," Joe said. "And look at you. Looks like you're up to the same."

"Naw," Freddie replied, "I left the business after my last stint."

"Really?" Joe said. "So what's the hustle?"

"No hustle," Freddie said, "I'm a new man. I have a ministry just off of Polk called Christ's Light for the Lost. You should come on by."

"Just might. Just might," Joe said. "I thought Glide Memorial, though, was big enough for this whole area."

"Glide has its place and followers," Freddie said, "and they do great work, but I'm down for the street, poverty and drug-infirm. For those who don't have the strength to make their way down from my end of the Tenderloin, to Glide on the opposite end. Speaking of those down on their luck, how'z my old girls Shelly and Kelly?" Freddie asked. "I sometimes wonder what happened to them after you pulled them out from my dark days. Are they still around?"

Joe looked up at me. There still was a bit of tension between me and Joe on the subject of Kelly. I believe he felt I had led her astray and got her mixed into things that were over her head. I was under the contention that yes, I may have gotten her involved, but there were choices that she made which resulted in her being in her current situation.

"Last time I checked," I said, "Kelly is doing time. And Shelly has some sort of business venture going." I left the part out that Shelly's business was an explicit video service and Kelly's time was connected with me.

"Too bad," Freddie said, looking at me and nodding. "That's too bad, but there's worse. Next time you get in contact with either of them, send them my way."

"Will do," I assured him and now Freddie seemed to recognize me, and he smiled and said, "Thanks."

Steve and Ozzie now stepped out of the office and strode over to where Freddie was standing, crowding him from behind. Freddie responded by an over exaggeration of shaking his shoulders, as if he was shaking off hands that were placed upon him. "Hold on fellas, give a guy some space." He laughed.

"Freddie," Joe said, "these are some of our newest employees, Steve and Ozzie."

Freddie, turned to face them and said, "Welcome to the neighborhood, boyz." He outstretched his hand and both Steve and Ozzie wiped their hands on their shirts before taking Freddie's, who laughed as he shook theirs.

MONDAY MORNING, AND I awoke late to little furry paws massaging the back of my neck; Poseidon, my orange tabby, was hungry and decided it was time for me to climb out of bed and feed him. As a rule, he's normally kept out of my bedroom, but lately I've been waking up finding him in the room with me and sometimes he wakes me up with morning massages. I haven't quite figured out how he does it. Maybe he sneaks in the night before, for sometimes the door is still closed in the morning when I get up.

I carried Poseidon downstairs and made him breakfast and made myself a cup of coffee. I gathered my bills from the night before and placed them in my pocket, envisioning a trip to the post office prior to stopping by the office. Poseidon, sated with dry kibble, was intent on cleaning himself on a kitchen chair and paid no attention to my departure that would leave him to do what cats do when no one is home: sunbathe, chase bugs, play solitaire.

Outside, the clouds had broken, signaling the latest storm had moved on its merry way to wreak havoc in other people's lives as it made its week-long track across the US. Little did I realize, however, a different kind of deluge had been released upon the residents of Pacifica.

It had started as a trickle over the weekend and by the time I decided to head to the post office prior to heading to work on Monday morning, it was already a torrent. I had left my townhouse on Oddstad and climbed over the hill to catch Terra Nova Blvd, which is the quickest way to the Linda Mar post office on Roberts Road. When I reached Terra Nova I found it strange that I ran into traffic, being traffic is only on this road for a short period during Terra Nova High School start and end times, or if there is an evening football game. I slowly crept up Terra Nova, expecting Fassler Avenue to ease things up, as it opens to two lanes, but it didn't.

Something was happening down on Highway One. Traffic was stop and go and just inching along. When I came to the Roberts Road turnoff that leads to the Linda Mar Post office, I took it and noticed an unusual amount of cars parked on the side of the road. People were out of their cars, pointing out from the cliff side of Robert's Road towards Pacifica Beach and Highway One. When I spotted my neighbor Cathy Mays out on one of the bluffs along Robert's Road with her dog Rover, I decided to pull over myself and take a look.

"Isn't this exciting?" Cathy said as I came up alongside her. "Gold—they found gold here in Pacifica!"

I groaned. Arthur had wasted no time in getting the word out to whip up the masses into a gold hunting frenzy. "How long has this been going on?" I asked.

"Haven't you read the paper of late? Watched the news?" Cathy asked in surprise.

"Can't say that I have," I said. And I hadn't. I normally find television news too depressing or it winds me up so I can't sleep.

"Well, someone found a whole bunch of gold coins down on the beach and now everyone is looking. Some say there is a treasure somewhere here in Pacifica. Pacifica! Can you imagine! And it may be worth millions of dollars!"

From the ridge that makes Roberts' Road, overlooking Highway One and Pacifica Beach, we had the perfect vantage point to watch the chaos that was unfolding as people rushed to find more coins. Police were at the intersections but it didn't appear to be doing any good. What looked like a hippie van had broken down on Highway One and seemed to just compound the chaotic atmosphere. Amateur fortune seekers were already scouring the beach and the hill that separates Pacifica Beach from Rockaway Beach.

"Looks like Rockaway is probably just as packed," I said to Cathy.

"Isn't this exciting!" she squealed.

"It's a madhouse out there," I said. I found it depressing. Traffic jams and chaotic mass hordes. That's something I now associated with San Francisco. To see it in my adopted hometown was depressing.

"Can't be locals," I said. I took a look around to see who was up on the ridge with us, looking down at the chaotic scene. Some people I recognized, though I didn't know their names. Grocery store employees, people I see around town. No one seemed to stand out, except for one person.

Standing on the bluff down the hill from me and looking quite amused was a woman who was dressed as if she had stepped out of one of the Raiders of the Lost Ark movies. Tall and fit, wearing a brown Australian outback hat, auburn hair cascading down her back, her khaki shirt matching her khaki pants that were tucked into a pair of Columbia hiking boots—her outfit so amused me that I chuckled, excused myself from Cathy, and then headed over to where this woman was standing to take a closer look at her.

As I approached, I could see her bemused look change as her eyes caught sight of me. Coolly, she set her focus back to the chaotic gold hunting mess below her.

"Pretty funny isn't it," I said as I sidled up to her.

She turned to look back at me. "Funny," she replied.

She then looked me up and down like a specimen, so I decided to oblige. I outstretched my arms parallel to the ground and asked, "Should I turn?

"Yes." She smiled.

I slowly turned. "Still funny?" I asked.

"No," she replied. "I'd say good. Quite good." She smiled and I smiled back. She then caught my eyes as they drifted down, catching the chain around her neck. The chain held a large gold nugget and rested in her cleavage.

"Nice," I said.

"This really isn't me," she said, pointing at the nugget, "These are," she laughed as she grabbed her own breasts, "but this isn't," she said, lifting the nugget so I could inspect it.

"I hadn't made a decision on either," I said.

"If you look the part, you find more doors are open for you," she said. "If you look like you mean business. There are plenty of Johnny-Come-Lately's out here." She motioned to the crowd below.

"Business," I said. "You've made a business out of . . ."

"I scrape a living by treasure hunting," she interjected.

"Hmm," I said as I joined her in looking at the treasure hunters below.

"You do know they're looking in the wrong place," she said, motioning her head to the people down below, "but they'll catch on. In no time, someone will start scouring the creeks, followed by another and another."

"I guess you have it already figured out," I said.

"I have some thoughts on the subject," she said.

"Care to share them with me?" I asked.

"Now why would I want to do that?" She raised an eyebrow.

"Well, I might have some inside information you might not be aware of," I replied.

"Really," her eyes flared. "Care to share that with me?" She smiled now, seductively.

"Over drinks?" I invited.

"Sure," she replied. "Follow you?"

"Naw," I said. "Let's just take a walk down the street a bit to the Pacifica Beach Resort hotel, where we can have a drink and watch the craziness."

"Sure thing," she replied. "Let me just lock up."

I followed her to her white Mercedes Sprinter van. It was one of the most elaborate and completely outfitted vehicles I had seen in a long time, filled with compartments and shelves, a little table, chair, laptop and a half dozen antennas on the roof.

"Got a bed in there?" I smirked.

"Of course," she said matter-of-factly. She closed the back doors of her van and padlocked it. We then walked the short distance to the hotel, entering through the back.

The Pacifica Beach Resort hotel, located on a little knob of a hill at the corner of Crespi Drive, Highway One and Roberts Road, contains multiple octagon shaped buildings that cascade down to the hotel's main entrance. The hotel, with its red roofed buildings, panoramic windows and white trim, looks like something right out of a Thomas Kinkade painting.

Right off of the main entrance, the hotel has a large bar and restaurant with its floor to ceiling windows looking out onto Crespi Drive, Highway One and Pacifica Beach. We made our way to a little table in the corner of the bar and quickly a short Hispanic waitress took our orders for Bloody Marys. We sat in silence for a few moments, taking in the bar's ambiance, watching the people outside; the local cop directing traffic, pointing and yelling for people to move this way or that and getting comfortable sitting across from each other.

Our drinks arrived and I started. "So," I said, "I don't believe I caught your name."

This Indiana Jones looking woman straightened in her seat, turned a bit as if to get a better view up Highway One, but was in reality giving me a profile of herself. She took the stick of celery in her drink and made a little vortex in the concoction.

"Interesting," I said.

"What?" she said.

"You," I replied. "Interesting how you are trying to figure out what to tell me."

"I'm deciding something," she said.

"What?" I asked.

"Deciding if I should give you my business name," she said, "or my real name."

"Why not both?" I said.

"Okay," she said, "My real name is Rochelle. Rochelle Fortune, but for my business, I go by Rich Fortune."

"Rich Fortune!" I laughed, "Oh that's great!" I clapped.

She turned red. "I knew I might get a reaction like that out of you," she said. "That's why I was hesitant. It works though," she said, "for the business."

"So how's business?" I smirked. "Ms. Rich Fortune."

"Surprisingly . . . ," she paused and faced me, awaiting an answer.

"Mike," I replied and put out my hand, which she took, "Mike Mason."

She seemed agreeable. "Surprisingly, Mike, it is doing well." She continued, "It's all about research and finding the backing. Yes, I can say I've done well, real well, and so much so that I now have pretty much what I can call a permanent backer who may get a whiff of something, then sends me out to wherever to check things out. I do the research, find if anything is worth investing time and money, and let things go from there."

"Lost shipwrecks, anything along those lines?" I asked.

"More like mining," she said, "I pore over maps, historical information, try to piece the story of an area together, and yes, I do some archaeological stuff on both land and sea. I do like to get my hands dirty."

"Unlike me," I said, showing her my clean and just manicured hands. "Don't like getting my hands dirty."

A car skidded to a stop at the intersection below us. The red-faced cop was pointing with one hand, yelling something to a driver in a hippie van, while waving for a surfer carrying a bright yellow board to cross the street.

"Something about the word 'gold' gets people to go numb nuts," Rochelle said, motioning towards the crowd of people outside. "Normal, everyday people drop what they are doing and head for the hills. It has happened over and over again throughout history. So strange." We both watched the surfer make it to the other side of the street, shaking his head as he walked pass the van that had slammed on their brakes. "So Mike," Rochelle continued, "what do you, and your clean hands, do?"

"I'm an office jockey," I replied. I normally refrain from telling people that I'm a detective, if we just met. I've found in the past that many immediately give me the stink eye and go on the defensive, as if I would immediately go about the work of trying to uncover something they have hidden about their life.

"What sort of work?" Rochelle asked.

I leaned back in my chair and took a long look at Rochelle. She seemed like a down-to-earth woman, someone I could be straight with and who wouldn't give me the stink eye.

"Interesting," Rochelle said.

"How so?" I asked.

"Now you're deciding what you should tell me," she said.

I smiled and gave in. "All right," I said, "I'm actually a detective."

"Police?" She asked.

"Private." I replied.

"Really?" Rochelle said, perking up and leaning across our table. "Then we actually have a lot in common."

"How so?" I asked.

"We both enjoy piecing together puzzles. Putting together the missing pieces to get a clearer picture of our world," Rochelle said. "It is all about solving mysteries."

"Agreed," I said.

"Solving mysteries such as this one. The one about the gold coins." Rochelle pushed to the reason we were currently sharing our time.

"Such as this one," I repeated.

"You said you had some information," Rochelle stated. "What kind of information?"

I took a long, slow sip of my Bloody Mary and set the glass back down on the table. "A friend of mine," I said as I spun my glass on its moisture ring, "was the one who found the coin."

"Think you'll be able to get him to show it to me?" Rochelle asked, leaning toward me.

"Right now he does not have the coin in his possession," I said, thinking Joe had probably taken it to the museum to get it verified.

Rochelle's brow furrowed and for the first time I could see that she had some strength that complemented her rugged outfit. "Well, is there anything more you can tell me that wasn't in the newspapers and the news?" She sounded annoyed.

"I didn't catch the story in the media." I confessed. "Sort of a recluse that way. Tell me the gist of what you've heard and I'll fill in the gaps."

Rochelle recounted the story Joe had laid out in the bar the previous week, and that Arthur had printed in his paper. Arthur had also listed the many shipwrecks that had happened along the coast and how most of their remaining cargo that wasn't salvaged at the time, was possibly now a buried treasure that could be just beneath the shifting sands.

Arthur had also alluded that much more gold was probably out there, Armando's gold, somewhere on the beach, brought up by the recent storms, just waiting to be scooped up by the determined, observant, or just lucky. It was classic Arthur McCoy.

"That pretty much covers everything I know thus far," I said once Rochelle had finished recounting what she had read, "and then some."

Rochelle leaned into her chair and stared at me for a few moments in contemplation and examination, sizing me up. I sat back in my chair, slowly taking a sip of my drink and staring right back at her. She finally adjusted herself in her seat and asked, "So Mike, being that I'm not familiar with the area, what might a native of Pacifica like yourself show a visitor such as myself as local landmarks?"

"Transplant," I said, "San Francisco transplant."

"What would someone with a keen eye such as yourself," Rochelle continued, "show to someone such as myself?"

I pondered this for a moment, then, looking through the glass window behind Rochelle and across the street into the parking lot of the Senior Services Center, I found my first sight.

"Well," I said, "if you look out over your shoulder—see that statue across the street, that?" I said. "That is a statue of Gaspar de Portola." Rochelle turned around and took a long look then turned back to face me.

"Normally statues near the ocean look out to sea," she said. "Seems to me like he is facing the wrong way."

"I thought that as well, but then you have to remember, he is arriving on these shores. He's not looking at where he came from, wanting to get out of here, he is looking inland, at the area he is going to explore."

"Is that it?" Rochelle asked.

"Hmmm, what else, what else." I pondered. "Well, there's a stone marker up on top of Sweeny Ridge, near a Nike Missile site that marks the spot where the first non-native, one of Portola's expedition party, first laid their eyes on San Francisco Bay. There's also a marker just off of 280 that marks a Portola campsite on their trek."

My mind was now on a roll. "There is Sam's castle that was once a speakeasy, and there's the Sanchez Adobe."

"Sanchez Adobe?" Rochelle broke in. "That place was mentioned in the paper."

"Oh yeah," I said. "Do you want to visit it?"

"Yes, definitely," Rochelle said.

I checked my watch. "I don't think they are open right now," I said. "It's either a state or county park. Budget cuts, you know. Limited hours and days. I can check it out, though, and give you a call later."

"Sure," Rochelle said. "You have a card?"

We exchanged business cards and ordered another round when the waitress dropped by.

"So what else is there to see?" Rochelle asked.

"Well of historical interest," I said, "I guess there's the Little Brown church. I don't know much about it, but I know they are always raising money for its upkeep. Other than that," I shrugged, "it's all about nature here. Great beaches, hiking trails everywhere, a golf course."

"Any night life?" she asked.

"Psh," I said. "We have the premier bowling alley along the coast, Sea Bowl. Other than that, there's a bunch of bars, karaoke at most of them, a wine bar, maybe dancing to the oldies at Nick's—other than that, there isn't much besides walking the pier. Your best bet is heading into the city; it's only twenty minutes away."

Rochelle looked at me for awhile then said, "It sounds, though, like you still really like this place."

I paused for a moment as our drinks arrived. "It takes awhile to get used to," I said. "Hope I don't sound like someone who just discovered a new religion. I still love the city, but Pacifica does have its charms."

We both took gratuitous helpings of our drinks. "So, a change of subject," I said. "Where are you from and how did you get into treasure hunting business?"

"Everywhere and nowhere," Rochelle said. "Born and raised in West Virginia. My dad was a miner. Got into it from his daddy. So it's a family quest, I guess you can say."

"Didn't catch an accent," I said.

"Yowl mean you expectin me to talk like dis when I talk 'bout my daddy?" Rochelle said putting on a thick West Virginian accent.

"Exactly," I laughed and clapped my hands.

"How 'bout you?" Rochelle asked, "What got you into the detective business?"

"Just basically answered an ad in the paper and started from the ground up," I said. "But I guess there is something in my blood as well. My dad was a cop in San Francisco. Mean son of a bitch. Wanted me to be a cop as well. Closest I got to bucking him, I guess, was becoming a private investigator. I remember him saying P.I.'s were scum. His dad, my grandfather, was a P.I. in the City and I guess they had a falling out."

Rochelle's cell phone went off and she put up a finger that said 'hold that thought'. She climbed out of her chair and walked some distance away from me so I couldn't hear her conversation. When she returned, she didn't sit down and looked a little hurried. "I have to make some phone calls," she said, "run around, get some things done."

She must have seen a look on my face, for she jumped in before I could say anything. "Want to show me around some of those locations and places you mentioned?"

"Sure," I replied.

"Great," she replied, sounding all business. "Call me later when you have a day and time and we can go to Sanchez Adobe."

"All right," I said. "Will do."

I took a final swig of my drink, paid the bill and we headed out the back of the hotel and up to our vehicles. We said our goodbyes at her van and I watched her take off down Roberts Road. I arrived at my car and decided to take one last look at the mayhem below. From where I stood, I could see the Highway One northbound traffic heading out of Pacifica was moving freely and in it, I could see Rochelle's white Sprinter van rushing toward San Francisco.

WEEK II

A WEEK HAD PASSED SINCE we had moved into our Tenderloin office, so I needed to check in on Steve's progress. I also wanted to check in on Ozzie. It's probably not the best practice to leave an intern in charge, but at the moment, we were stretched pretty thin. It was a Tuesday afternoon so Ozzie was scheduled to be in at our Marina office, which is located in the Union Street Plaza Building at the corner of Union and Buchanan. I never liked that building. Esthetically, being a giant block of gray, brick, metal, and glass, it doesn't fit in the neighborhood of generally brightly colored one story buildings, but the rent is relatively cheap for the area and with a parking garage, it wasn't too annoying that I felt the urge to prod Joe to have us move out.

I took the puke green elevator from the garage to the second floor and when the doors opened, I immediately heard gunfire. Not just gunfire, but gunfire with heavy artillery. Someone was playing some sort of video game. I walked over to our office. The sounds were coming from inside, and I could see Ozzie facing the television, his body twisting and contorting as he worked a video game controller. I quietly opened the office door, then slammed the door behind me.

Ozzie jumped in his seat, then fell backwards and to the floor as his swivel chair careened across the office. I started laughing as the television screen turned bright red, then dark red, and then black as words written in white appeared, "You are dead!" Ozzie's game was over.

"Jeez, Mike!" Ozzie said. "You almost gave me a heart attack.

"Worse," I said, nodding toward the television screen. "I killed you."

Ozzie straightened himself up and retrieved his chair. "Sorry," he apologized. "I know I shouldn't have been playing."

"Look, I'm not blaming you," I said. "It's partly my fault. We've pretty much left you out here on your own as our business is changing, but you need to understand—how can I sign off on your progress reports for your proctor if all you are doing is using your time here to play video games?"

Ozzie nodded, keeping his head down.

"Listen," I said, "I'm dropping over to see Steve next. By now he should have things in order over there, or close to it. I'll have him hook up with you and he can give you some tips on computer sleuthing and doing the background checks for our regular customers. In the meantime . . ." I went over to one of the filing cabinets, pulled out a couple of manila folders, each folder a client's case, and took out the cover sheet from each file which listed the basics of the case, and handed them to Ozzie.

"Take a look at these," I said. "These were the most recent cases that were generated from this office and resolved. I want you go over these sheets and list what Internet sources you would have tapped to get the necessary information to move on to resolve these cases.

These are still relatively new, so they are still fresh in my head. Give me a holler if you have any questions about the cases and I'll walk you through. If you get stuck or can't find any sources, give Steve a call. He should be able to keep you on track. I want a full report next week."

I walked over to the gaming console and pressed a couple of buttons before finding the one that opened it. I retrieved the gaming disc from inside the device. "You won't be needing this for awhile." I placed the disc in my pocket and took the three files with me, leaving Ozzie just with their case cover sheets.. "Talk to you later," I said as I left the office.

When I left our Marina branch, I wasn't mad. It was natural for Ozzie to be goofing off. He was still a kid and was unsupervised. But it was something I would have to get on Steve about. Ozzie was to be his charge while he learned the ropes.

I drove up Lombard and climbed Russian Hill, making a right onto Hyde, to slide along the cable car tracks for a few blocks. I then made a left onto Union and a right onto Jones so as I passed Green Street, I could catch a glimpse of the Spite Building. I slowed my car to glance at the building that once housed a woman that touched my life. I didn't stop though, and continued down Jones and headed over to the Tenderloin.

The parking in the Tenderloin is always an iffy proposition. If you find a spot, you may come back and find your car missing, stolen, towed, or vandalized, even if the police station is across the street from you. So I took a spot in the lot at Taylor and O'Farrell and then walked the three blocks to our office.

When I arrived at our doorway, I found my entrance blocked, not by the security gate, which I asked to be left open during business hours, which it was, but blocked by the nasty, absolutely nasty smells wafting out from our doorway. Indeed, the whole area smelled like an overflowing toilet. It had smelled bad when we first looked into moving into the place, the slight scent of vomit and urine, but nothing like it smelled now. Obviously some of the neighborhood regulars had taken it upon themselves to welcome us in their own way. Our floor, walls and door entrance were completely stained with urine.

I tried our front door and found that it was locked as I started to gag from the assault on my sense of smell. I slide my key into the lock, retrieved my hankerchief to grab the door handle, and let myself in. "What the fuck?" I said when I entered. Steve was in the back of the office. Piles upon piles of boxes were open, files scattered about, cabinet doors open.

"Hey Mike!" Steve said. "What's the matter?"

"What's the matter?" I said, still pissed at the gauntlet of acrid smells I had to pass through to enter the office. "Just look at this place."

"I know, I know," Steve said. "Just organizing. Hey, did you know that Joe's dad was murdered back in 1970? It looks like the case was never solved."

"Yes I know," I said, walking over to him, snatching the file from his hand, looking at it, then closing it and placing it on top of a nearby cabinet. "And don't you know that the majority of these files are now at least ten plus years old, with some going back to the 1930s? They're here just so we don't have to pay storage. Just stack 'em and leave them be."

"Even the one on Mr. Thomas Ballard, Joe's father?"

"Especially that one," I said. "There's absolutely no reason to spend your time digging up old bones when you have a current job to do."

"Something came in?" Steve asked.

"You're the one who should be telling me if something has come in," I replied. "Look Steve," I continued, "I know you, you're a good guy, and a hell of a great researcher on the Internet, but we have you here to re-establish our presence in the neighborhood. I know you feel more comfortable behind a computer screen, but if that is all we wanted, we would have left you in the Marina. You can do internet searches from anywhere. What we want is a presence in the community. We want to be seen, to be out there. You won't see anything if you're locked in the office. Here, this is my mission for you. Every morning, pick up a coffee somewhere, at a different place every couple of days, and then go back again to ones you've been to in a couple of weeks. Go out and eat at the local restaurants. Walk the neighborhood. Pick up a Coke at the liquor store and buy cigarettes often. You'll see that cigarettes are a commodity down here and will get people talking as you provide them one to light up. I want you to know the streets like the back of your hand, the alleys. Know all the massage parlors, bars, restaurants and liquor stores. Get to know the garbage men and the local police. And get to know the myriad of groups that come down here to help lift people up, the shelters and all. Get their numbers and have them handy, where you can give them as referrals. We need you to be a friend of the community, a part of the community and that is how to make things easy when a job comes your way."

The sunlight entering through our smoky front door glass shifted with the presence of someone entering our doorway. It caught my attention, as did the thought that a potential new client was about to come through our front door. The shadow in the doorway looked like the person was reaching down toward the door handle, though the time it was taking him to try the handle brought the thought that he was possibly covering his hand with a handkerchief as I had done before grabbing hold of it. That was my thought until I heard the distinct sound of someone taking a piss.

"Give me your Barbie!" I demanded.

"My what?" Steve asked.

"Your gun! Give me your goddam gun!"

Steve frantically pulled at a desk drawer, reached inside and handed me a gun, butt first. I grabbed it, marched over to the front door, opened it, and grabbed the pisser by his collar and yanked him inside. I swung him around and up against the wall. He was drug thin, ashy white, unkempt, and smelled of a combination of alcohol and crack. I put the barrel of my gun in his mouth and made sure it clicked against his teeth.

"I guess you're not from around here," I said, hoping I was yelling loud enough and being aggressive enough to break through his drug fog to make an impression. "If you were, you would have known that the large green box at the corner and across the street, right next to the park, is a public toilet and it costs just twenty-five cents to use. Or I can guess that you are from around here and can't afford the quarter. But let me just tell you, it is not all right, hear me, it is not all right that you find the need to relieve yourself in my doorway, on my building, on my block! So what I want you to do, from here on out, is to take your sorry ass and find another place to take a piss. I don't care if it is in the street, or in another doorway. Just not here! And if I ever catch you or any of your compadres doing so, in my doorway, the next time they take a piss will be from a tube at General!"

I put Steve's gun in my waistband, then pulled the guy to the front door, opened it, and kicked him out of the office, where he fell to the curb. I relocked the front door.

"I thought you said I had to be nice and get to know these people?" Steve smirked as I handed him his gun to place it back into the drawer.

"Sometimes you also just need to claim your territory," I said as I walked to the back of the office to wash my hands clean in our small lavatory. "And there's also a hierarchy out here. We just jumped a couple of rungs of the ladder." I dried my hands and looked under the sink.

"No worries that he'll run to the cops and tell them you pulled a gun on him?" Steve asked.

"Out here?" I called from the bathroom. "Won't happen. If he had any street cred, that would take it away. Anyway, whose story would the cops believe, some crackhead who just got threatened for pissing on a business, or the business owner?" I headed out of the bathroom, "Don't worry, kid," I said, "you'll learn." I went up to Steve and pulled out a ten. "Go out and get some bleach to toss on our doorway."

When Steve left on the errand, I went to the file we had on Joe's father, Tom Ballard. It was thick, but it was already an old and cold case by the time I had entered the picture. I looked at the picture of Tom that was inside his case folder. He was a spitting image of what Joe looked now. If it was Joe in the folder, I wondered, would I ever close the case and leave it as unsolved, or would I continue working on it years later? I opened a cabinet door and placed the file inside.

A COUPLE OF MORE DAYS passed before I was able to get hold of Rochelle again, and when I finally did get hold of her, although the Sanchez Adobe was open during the week, Rochelle was not free during those times until Friday. So we made plans to go to the adobe on Friday and connected the rest of the week, either in the morning for a coffee or late afternoon for a quick bite, then a drive or hike around the area.

My days during this time were relatively free. Normally this time of year, things would be hopping down at the office. The old springtime birds and the bees things, where all the primeval urgings seem to stir from their winter sleep and get people into trouble. Normally a client every other day, week in, week out, arrives in our Pacifica branch or our Marina branch, men and women, with tears in their eyes and a story to tell. But not this week. It was quiet except for the noise about gold.

With so much time on my hands, I actually picked up a copy of the Coastal Watch, the rag that Arthur writes for, and began reading it.

On the front page was another story by the illustrious Arthur McCoy. In this story, Arthur reported on the mad rush of fortune seekers and how they were degrading the area, how the marshlands of the creek were being trampled underfoot as exemplified by a woman who found a man digging a hole out of the creek bank that formed part of her backyard. The man's digging resulted in a slump of dirt to move from the homeowner's yard and into the creek. All the tramping around the creek also endangered the steelhead that spawned in the creeks. Environmentalists were in an uproar and Arthur was sure to be fanning the flames. Whip them up into a frenzy for gold, and then whip them up into a frenzy about gold from a different angle. I had to hand it to Arthur; he was good at his job.

I had just finished reading the story when Joe came into the office. "Ahhh. Shit," Joe said. "It's getting too crazy down there."

Joe was looking a bit disheveled. His straw hat was cockeyed, his shirt dirty, his pants ripped below his knee. "What the hell happened?" I asked.

"Ahh," Joe said as he sat down in his chair, outstretching the leg with the ripped pants, "I got a beep and this guy knocked me over into the rocks and started sweeping the area with his detector. Sliced me pretty good." Joe bent to grab his leg then sat back in his chair. "But I got him back, though. Used my detector to bang his leg up, then pushed him into the surf. The ignorant dumbass!"

"You all right?" I asked. "Want a bandage?"

"No," Joe said, "I'm okay."

I got out of my chair and headed to the back of the office anyway, to get him a couple of bandages and some Neosporin from a little blue emergency kit we keep in the bathroom.

"So haven't seen you in awhile," Joe called from the front of the office. "What have you been up to?"

"Hold on," I yelled back. I just grabbed the entire medical kit and when I returned, I found Joe massaging his right thigh.

"Thanks," Joe said as I opened the kit and handed it to him. "These were some damn good pants. So what have you been up to?" he repeated. "Haven't seen you around for a couple of days. Didn't look like we had any outstanding jobs or new clients. And how'z things with Steve and Ozzie? Have you checked in with them?"

"Yeah, I'm keeping an eye on 'em," I said, though in reality, I had only dropped in on them that one time since the move. "Things are coming along. And I've been doing a little bit of gold hunting myself with one of your competitors," I said and Joe stopped rifling through the medical kit. "Well not actually," I smiled. "Been more of a tour guide for Pacifica."

"Who is he?" Joe asked.

"Not a he," I said, "a she."

"Really?" Joe reached into a desk drawer and pulled out a large black handled scissor and began to cut his pants leg above the knee. "Damn good pair of pants," he said with a tinge of remorse.

"Some woman I just met a couple of days ago," I said. "Name of Rich Fortune."

Joe stopped cutting his pants and I watched as his face turned as he tried to remember something, then he resumed, finished the cut, slipped off his shoe and kicking off the severed pant leg. "Any luck finding anything?" Joe asked as he began to clean up his scraped knee with an alcohol wipe.

"I don't think she's gotten her feet yet." I continued, "Still scoping out the tale of Armando's gold. Trying to figure out what is true and what is legend."

"Oh, it is true," Joe said as he applied some Neosporin, followed by some cotton gauze. "All of it."

"Well she's going about it another way," I said in her defense.

"You know," Joe said, "I think I've heard of her before; a story about her in the LMM, the Loco Mining Magazine. Some article about her awhile back. Rich Fortune." Joe began to take the scissors to his left pant leg, "Yeah, that's right, something about her being a treasure hunting predator."

"Treasure hunting predator?" I laughed, "Didn't know there was such an animal."

"I think there's a lawsuit," Joe said as he continued cutting. "Claims of her undercutting a site, blackmail and murder for a big claim up near Placerville. Her and her partner."

"Partner?" I said. "She hasn't mentioned anyone else, but she does take a lot of calls that I'm not privy to. Hey," I said, "I'm supposed to hook up with her later today. Over at Sanchez Adobe. Want to come along?"

"What time?" Joe said as he kicked off his left pant leg.

"Around two." I said.

Joe stood up. "Ahhh, can't today. I'm doing some cooking at the Moose Lodge this evening," he said. "Need to start early preparation; a Friday Fundraiser dinner."

Joe put his hands on his waist and I could easily see his homemade shorts had been cut crooked and were uneven. "How do I look?" He asked.

"Peachy," I said, "Just peachy."

Joe smirked. "You can join in and give us a hand. Stick around for a free steak dinner if you have nothing going on after your meeting with Rich."

"Maybe," I said. "If I have a chance, I'll drop by."

"Sure," Joe said. "Sure."

I ARRIVED AT SANCHEZ ADOBE at exactly one-fifty to find Rochelle waiting. The grounds of this county historical park are immaculate, even with the countywide cutbacks. We walked up a short dirt path, past a billboard that showed a calendar of upcoming events, and arrived at the front door of the adobe, where we were greeted by a man wearing a thick brown robe. He had brown eyes, jovial red cheeks, was about six-two, two hundred-fifty pounds and had thick mutton chops and a receding hairline. He was wearing sandals, the kind I always picture as Jesus shoes.

"Hello, hello, welcome to San Pablo y Asistencia." the man in the robe started, "I am Brother Daniel Burgos. Here we grow crops and then later, cattle in our support of the Mission San Francisco de Asis, later known as Mission Dolores in San Francisco. Follow me, my brothers and sisters."

Rochelle and I looked at each other, shrugged and followed him about a dozen feet from the entrance of the adobe to a section of field that had logs laid out to form squares and rectangles.

"What you see before you is the location of the foundations for San Pablo y Asistencia, which was built to support Mission Dolores in San Francisco in way of food and converts." Brother Daniel continued, "There was a chapel here as well as a granary. It was a largely farming outpost, until there was a dramatic decline in the native population that coincided with the Mexican War of Independence from Spain, during which it became mostly a cattle ranch."

Daniel turned towards the adobe and began walking. "Come on, let's head inside." We followed 'Brother Daniel' into the ground floor of the adobe and the main room.

"Now welcome to the home of Francisco Sanchez. Francisco Sanchez was the commandant of the San Francisco Presidio and was awarded in 1839 a large amount of land by the then Mexican Governor. That land grant included the mission lands of San Pablo y Asistencia, which had been long left to ruin and was confiscated by the Mexican government. Feel free to look around, check out the display cases. Ask me any questions. When you are ready, we will continue with our tour."

Rochelle and I toured the room, checking out the dioramas and glancing over the text. Display cases held artifacts found at the site: spurs, glassware, pottery, nails, horseshoes, cow bones and grinding stones. There were also drawings, maps, and pictures segregated by eras: Native, Mission, Mexican, and American. And of course, there was the ubiquitous collection of stuffed hand puppets, books and knickknacks to be sold to tourists by a cashier.

We wandered into the two adjacent rooms. One room was set up as a storage room filled with horse tack, barrels containing food, and onions and garlic which hung from the redwood beam ceiling. The other room was set up as a living space and contained a china cabinet, a fireplace, a small stove and a table with chairs. We returned to the main room and Daniel asked, "Done? Shall we continue upstairs?"

We agreed and followed him outside and then climbed the stairs to the second level and entered the rooms on the second floor. "After Francisco Sanchez passed away," Daniel continued, "the building was sold, foreclosed upon, and sold again in 1879 to General Edward Kirkpatrick, who extensively remodeled the structure, making it bigger then you currently see it. From then until 1946, when it was sold again, the adobe was used as a hotel, a house of prostitution, a speakeasy, as were so many places on the Coast, a hunting lodge, and a few other things as it slowly fell into disrepair. Finally, the county purchased the land and took up the restoration of the adobe. Here, take a look around."

The second floor was quite different from the first floor, being more finished and made into a home. One room had a bassinet, a small bed and dresser, a mannequin draped in a woman's nightgown and some chairs. The center room contained a piano, a small doily-draped round table and three chairs, a bookcase, another small square table and chairs that held a mock oil lamp, and a bench by the window. The third room contained a large bed, an armoire, another bassinet, two more mannequins with women's clothing, and a desk with a vanity. All three rooms were sectioned off using a black metal railing and the walls and ceiling looked sheet-rocked. After a quick scan of the place, Rochelle and I met up with Daniel, who was standing by the second floor door.

"So what about the native Americans?" Rochelle asked. "Where were they during this time?"

"Follow me," Daniel said. We followed Daniel onto the veranda, past the stairway down to the first level, and headed over to overlook the western side of the property. "Out there by my horse . . ." Daniel paused for us see where he was pointing.

I looked where I thought Daniel was motioning, but I didn't see a horse. I looked all around, didn't see one. I looked at Rochelle and she was straining her eyes. "I don't see no horse," she said, slipping into her West Virginia accent.

That was when I caught Daniel's reason for pausing. It was his inside joke. Daniel's horse was an old black Schwinn bicycle.

"Bike," I said to Rochelle and Daniel laughed.

"Yes," Daniel continued, "out by my horse, next to the ranger's building, was a shell midden. This area used to be the site of the Oholone village of Pruristac. They lived here in sort of woven buildings made of willow branches. They were basket makers and a hunting and gathering culture. Members of this village apparently met with Gaspar de Portola when he landed here, but the record doesn't really say if he ever ventured forth to this village."

"So," Rochelle said, "there was a native village here, then the Spanish missionaries came in and set up camp to convert the residents."

"San Pablo y Asistencia," I said and Daniel nodded.

"Then the Mexican War of Independence supplanted the Spanish and native Americans." Rochelle continued.

"Not being much of either group here by then," I interjected.

"And the land was given to this Francisco Sanchez by the Mexican governor at the time." Rochelle continued, "When he passed away, the land and building went thorough various hands and transformations, until it eventually ended up in the hands of the county."

"Correctimundo," Daniel said.

We stood in silence for a few moments, looking at the land below us, at the current buildings, envisioning life in the different eras. It was after that, I broke the silence and entertained the real reason we were there. "So what about this Armando fellow everyone is interested in lately?" I asked.

Daniel smiled. "And I thought you were interested in historical information."

"We are," Rochelle interjected and continued, "but isn't he a point of historical interest?"

"Not from what I can tell," Daniel said. "Everyone who has asked about him is just after gold. You all have gold fever."

"Or it's just human nature," I said.

Daniel shook his head. "We've been so dang plumb slammed with questions in regard to gold of late, and no one is interested in the facts, the real important history of this place."

Both Rochelle and I just stared at Daniel, and I guess he took it for it what it was worth. "Let's go back downstairs," Daniel said plainly. "There's a flyer that I made from doing research over at Mission Dolores. It has some quick facts about Amado."

"You mean Armando?" I corrected Daniel.

Daniel continued to walk down the stairs, the stairs creaking under his weight. "No, I mean Amado," Daniel sniped back.

"I've always heard that his name was Armando?" I replied as if I had been tossing the name Armando around the campfire for years. We re-entered the adobe on the ground floor.

"Most people say his name is Armando," Daniel said as he retrieved a brown rectangular brochure from a holder on a windowsill and handed it to me, "but he was also called Amado, as in Beloved, or God's Love."

I looked down at the brochure that Daniel had handed me. The title of the brochure was *Armando of Pacifica*. Below the title was a sketch of an old man wearing a ten gallon hat. He looked like pictures I've seen of gauchos. I reread the flyer's title out loud for Rochelle's benefit.

"Amado, I think that was his nickname," Daniel said. "Amado. Beloved. Who knows what he was called before either name was given to him. Many of the local Indians were just named Jose by the missionaries. He was lucky to get Armando."

Rochelle went around Daniel and retrieved a brochure for herself.

"From what I've gathered," Daniel continued, "he tried herding cattle for some of the families in the eighteen-seventies as he tried to purchase this land, after working at Mission Dolores. Never succeeded. Seems like he had the money, or at least sounds like he had gold, just never got it together, I guess."

I continued reading down the synopsis of Armando's life, or who I would call Amado in deference to Daniel. The synopsis condensed Amado's life to a four by eight brown rectangular piece of paper. "Ocean Shore Railroad," I commented to Rochelle as I read off Amado's bio that he was a frequent patron. "Never heard of it. Is that a train line from around here?" I asked Daniel. "Must be completely gone."

"Gone in the sense that it's not running," Daniel said, "but there are plenty of signs of it if you look around. Haven't you seen the bright orange rail car that is now Gorilla Barbeque? The red caboose that is P-Town coffee house and the old rail station that is a restaurant called Vallamar Station that is between the two?"

"I just figured . . ." I paused and thought about that area and corner of shops and restaurants. "I don't know what I figured."

I confessed and feeling bad for being put on the spot in front of Rochelle. "I just didn't think too much about it. Being originally from San Francisco, the thought of what was running down the Coast never was brought up much in my normal working conversations. And I've never seen any tracks down here. And with those train cars, I just thought it was like an easy way to make a building, or it was a gimmick or something."

Daniel stood tall, pleased that he was top history dog. He continued, reveling in his superiority on the subject matter, "Well, you're correct. The train cars over there wouldn't be from the Ocean Shore Railroad. Those were brought in. Vallamar Station however, that is a real train station from the Ocean Shore Railroad days. If you head farther down south, outside of Davenport, you can still see some tracks, a trestle, and a railroad tunnel that was made for the train line."

"Interesting. Really," Rochelle said. "It says Armando was a frequent rider."

"Not just a rider," Daniel said. "More like a fixture. From what I've heard from researching and talking to people, in his latter days, if he wasn't on the trains, he was outside one of the stations, watching the trains run in and out. He was there all the time."

"Hmm," I pondered, "A regular train buff."

Daniel looked us both up and down. "You two seem like nice people. If you like, I can get you in touch with someone who really knows some personal stuff about Amado. Are you interested?"

"Yes, of course," Rochelle jumped in. "Who?"

"Aw, a friend of mine," Daniel said. "His name is Moses Brown."

"Moses Brown," I repeated.

"Moses' grandfather actually knew Amado," Daniel said. "He was a coachman and would let Amado ride for free. If you go out to Vallamar Station, out on Highway One, between the railcar and caboose, you can still see a picture of Moses' grandfather inside the restaurant. In fact, the walls of the place are filled with pictures of the old Ocean Shore Railroad. If you are at all familiar with the coast, you can still pick out some of the landmarks in the pictures that show the rails or the train. You should really check it out."

"Yeah, we'll definitely check the place out," I said.

"What about Moses?" Rochelle said. "Can you get hold of him for us?"

"I can give him a call," Daniel said.

"We'll wait," Rochelle said, and I could see that Daniel was taken aback, so I decided to support her with, "Yeah, that would be great if you could get hold of him."

"All right, sure," Daniel said. "You have a phone I can use?"

"Sure," I said and handed him my cell.

Daniel stepped outside to make the call.

"Don't you think it is strange that he doesn't carry a cell of his own?" Rochelle asked. "Who doesn't have a cell?"

I pointed to the robe Daniel was wearing. "No pockets?" I guessed.

"Ah." Rochelle smiled.

When Daniel returned he gave me my phone and said, "Well, I left Moses a message to call your number and if he couldn't get it off his answering machine, for him to leave me a message at home."

"Great." I said, and then it struck me. "Oh I get it now," I said. "Something my buddy Joe had said was that part of the legend is that on the last day Amado was seen, he told one of the engineers that he had a great treasure hidden that he would give him. That was the Ocean Shore Railroad!"

"Didn't I read in the paper, per the legend," Rochelle said, "that gold was possibly buried here, and if not here, in a cave somewhere on Montara Mountain?"

"I'm sure you have," Daniel said, "but the thing is, the grounds here have been dug up many times over, for archaeological reasons. These grounds have been turned over and gone through with metal detectors—not for gold, mind you, but for artifacts of historical significance.

"What about in the adobe itself?" Rochelle asked. "Have you searched under the floors, in the foundations, in the furniture?"

"Now wouldn't that be something?" Daniel said, marveling at the space around him. "Well, if he had hid it in any furniture, it has been lost to antiquity. Pretty much all that you see here was brought in by the County. You have to remember, during and after Amado's time, this place changed hands multiple times and was everything from a bordello and hotel to a speakeasy and even an artichoke shed. When this place was purchased by the county in the late 1940s, it was pretty much gutted and the walls, floors and roof were in bad shape. Took the county and volunteers years to get this place to the point that you see it today."

"Any chance of anything being hidden in the foundation, floors or walls?" Rochelle asked.

Daniel paused. "Well, if there was, it is pretty much sealed away for good. Just look at these walls." Daniel placed a hand against the smooth surface on the inside of the adobe. "Cement," Daniel said.

"Cement?" Both Rochelle and I questioned.

"Again," Daniel said, "this place was falling apart when the County got it and well, back in the late forties, there weren't any established techniques in preserving things the way that we do now.

Basically, they did what they could. Did the best that they could at the time."

"But I . . ." Rochelle started, looking toward the adobe's door.

"Well, yes," Daniel said, "the outside of the building, the walls are pretty much structurally the original adobe, but inside is cement. And the eastern wall is fully cement. But all other external walls are the original adobe. The beams are all redwood and original as well."

"All right," I said. "Guess it's time to go. So say, if Moses calls you instead of me, how do you want us to contact you? Should we give you a call at your home or drop by here?"

"Oh yes," Daniel said. "Let me get your number. And you should really go over to Mission Dolores if you want to really find out about life of the Oholone Indians in general."

"I will," I assured him as I reached into my pocket, pulled out one of my business cards and handed it to Daniel. "Coastside Detectives, eh?' Daniel looked strangely at me, but he wasn't giving me the stink eye. "Would have been nice to have known you awhile back."

"For what?" I asked.

Daniel looked at Rochelle, then said, "It was a personal matter. Was taken care of."

"Well," I said, "our doors are always open." Daniel nodded in agreement. "And my real name is Daniel, Daniel Clay."

Rochelle had been looking at Daniel, studying him closely as we talked. "Thanks for all your help. You've been so kind. It's as if you really lived in the time of this place."

"I wish," Daniel said. "I try my best to live it, breathe it. Back then was another world. A simpler time. What's not to like? And well, as far as it is a job, my commute is a dozen blocks on my Schwinn. This is a great place to work." Daniel was smiling, then said, "Hey, we have something we call Rancho Day in the Fall every year. You should come on out. Authentic food is served and demonstrations of the various trades are performed with hands-on activities. You can dress up in period costumes. Become a regular local."

I smiled back at Daniel. He was being earnest. He really liked what he was doing, and I could tell he wanted us to attend the festival that he thought was great fun.

"In the Fall, you said?" I questioned.

"Yes. Normally around September or October," Daniel said

"I'll keep an eye out," I said as I exited the adobe through the front door.

"Sure," Daniel said. "Sure."

I did a double take, but Rochelle was right behind me and pushed me along. I continued walking past the adobe to the parking lot, but then realized Rochelle was no longer behind me. She was outside of the adobe, inspecting its walls. I headed back and met her at the western corner of the building. She was laying her hands on the adobe, her fingers touching the crevices between the bricks where dirt easily fell away and an adobe brick crumbled to the touch. "The key is still here," Rochelle said taking in a deep breath through her nose. "I can smell it."

F ROM THE PARKING LOT of Sanchez Adobe, Rochelle and I decided
to drive our vehicles the couple of blocks up to San Pedro County
Park and hike the in-and-out two mile Valley View trail. As we walked,
the back of one of her hands kept touching mine and at some point,
I just grabbed her hand and held it as we walked. She smiled, I smiled
and we walked to where the trail ended in a tiny meadow surrounded
by scrub brush and looped back upon itself. Here we stopped and
faced each other and kissed just as my phone began to ring.

The elderly sounding man on the other end of the line
identified himself as Moses. He said he would meet us around four in
the afternoon at the bar in Vallamar Station. I checked my watch and
started to calculate how much more time I could spend with Rochelle
but she said, "We should go," when I told her who had called.

When we finished our hike, it was close to four, so we drove
our separate vehicles to the Vallamar district of Pacifica, parked our

cars next to the P-Town coffee shop that is housed in a red caboose, and headed inside the Vallamar Station restaurant and bar.

Besides the normal bar embellishments of a neon rimmed clock, a neon Guinness sign, and a mechanical Budweiser sign containing Clydesdale horses making an endless circuit around a dim light, Vallamar Station had a banner over the bar announcing that there was karaoke at the bar on Friday nights from 9:30 to closing. I made note of that, always in search of another local venue to stretch my vocal cords.

Vallamar Station is also completely filled with memorabilia from the Ocean Shore Railroad. Signs of the train stops line the walls: Tunitas, Half Moon Bay, Granada, Moss Beach, Fallone, Montara, Tubin, San Francisco, Oceanview, Daly City, Salada, and Brighton.

At the bar, pieces of the railroad track are used as a footrest for the patrons. Two dioramas of the railroad, one of Vallamar Station, the other of the trestle around San Gregorio, which includes a shark and seals in the water below the train trestle, greet you in the foyer and immediate entrance of the bar. Picture frames cover the walls and are filled with historical pictures of the train, people and places along the Ocean Shore railroad track.

When we arrived, the bar itself was empty save for the bartender and a couple of waitresses, who all greeted us upon our arrival. You could, however, hear patrons in the back dining room and several people enjoying a leisurely drink around a fire pit on the outside patio. The bar itself was fairly well-lit inside, with a fireplace, red leather chairs, small round brown tables and one booth in a large alcove. After taking our time walking around, taking in the photos, Rochelle and I took a seat at the bar. I ordered a Jameson Manhattan, while Rochelle ordered a Cosmopolitan.

Around four-fifteen, a slim and well-dressed elderly black gentleman entered the bar, came up to us, and introduced himself.

"Hi," he said in a scratchy voice, "Your name wouldn't happen to be Mike Mason, would it now?"

I climbed off my stool as Rochelle spun around on her stool and partially rose to greet him.

"Yes I am." I said as I shook his hand. "And you must be Moses Brown."

"Yes sir, that I am." He then asked, "And who is this nice young woman?"

"Rochelle . . ." I began to say when Rochelle popped out of her seat and extended her hand. "Rich Fortune," she said. "So nice to meet you."

"Whoa, well!" Moses said excitedly as he became animated. "That's a great name!" he said, rocking from side to side. "I hope your name has brought you many riches and fortune!"

"It has," Rochelle said. "It has. And I'm even richer having met you."

"Well thank you kindly." Moses blushed, "As I am for meeting you."

"Here, let's move to one of the tables so we can all talk," I said. "Whatcha having?" I asked Moses as we grabbed a small table around the fireplace.

"Oh, that's so kind of you," Moses said. "Just a beer. A Budweiser."

I ordered Moses' beer and another round from one of the waitresses for Rochelle and myself and after some talk of the weather, Moses asked, "So how do you know Daniel?"

"We just met him today at Sanchez Adobe," I replied.

"Very nice man," Rochelle added, batting her eyes at Moses.

"How long have you known Daniel?" I asked.

"Me and him," Moses said, "ah, we goes way back. Maybe back around 1977. I knew his dad Frankie, from the Moose Lodge, and I was the one who directed him to work at the Adobe. Seemed like the perfect fit. He's quite a character, ain't he?"

"Yes he is," I smiled. "He was dressed up as a monk or something and played a little joke on us."

Moses started laughing, rocking in his chair as he slapped his thigh. "That's him, all right! Always out having a good time. Gonna have to drop by to see him. Especially now, with all that trouble . . ."

"What kind of trouble?" I asked as the waitress brought Moses his beer.

Moses turned somber as he took a drink. "Ah poor guy," Moses said. "Him and his wife. They be having some trouble as late. Things weren't going along too well, so he got the idea to hire that detective agency down in the Linda Mar shopping center a couple of months back." Rochelle looked over to me and I shook my head 'no' and decided he must have worked with Joe. Moses continued, "Had his wife followed for a bit. Turns out she was doing some guy up over on Grizzly. Became a real mess. He now spends most of his time at the Adobe. Says it's his sanctuary. He told me that sometimes now he sleeps there." Moses shook his head and began to peel the label off his bottle of Bud. His eyes were watery.

Rochelle reached across the table and squeezed one of his hands. "Sorry," she whispered.

I decided to change the subject. "So Daniel told us you might be able to tell us something about the old Indian named Amado?"

"He was probably more commonly known as Armando," Rochelle added.

"Yes, that's right." Moses said, smiling and squeezing Rochelle's hand back before letting it go to take a swig of his beer. "I know him as Armando."

"How do you know him, or rather, know about him?" I asked.

"Well, I never met him myself," Moses said. "Too old. Way before my time. But my grandpappy, he knew him. He knew him well. Used to see him almost daily for a time. I remember my grandpappy say he looked older than dirt. Wouldn't be surprised if he was two hundred years old, but we all know that couldn't be." Moses looked to us and Rochelle and I both shook our heads in agreement. He took another drink of his beer and continued.

"My grandpappy was a porter on the Ocean Shore railroad back in the day when it was running. He said he remembered seeing this old Injun that hung out at the train stations and would tell tales to the tourists for change or a lick of whiskey."

"So he was broke?" I asked. "Thought all these tales about him was that he had gold, piles of it somewhere."

"Well, yes," Moses continued, "he had some gold, some of it now and again. How much, I wouldn't rightly know. I never met him, just words from my grandpappy. Said he would disappear now and again, show up with some gold coins. Would sell some now and again. Would give some away now and again, but eventually he would run out and get to begging off the railroad for awhile. Near the end, when the train was running and coming to an end, seemed he had a lot less, as he was begging along the railroad for much longer periods of time."

"So maybe he had a small amount of gold and rumors, time and legend made it into a vast treasure," Rochelle stated.

"Well, he had enough at one time at least to try to buy the Adobe out there, ah, back in 1871. What I remember my grandpappy saying is that they refused to sell it to the Injun so he went to squatting the land somewhere out there. That is, until The Bank of America foreclosed on the landowner at that time and he was forced to leave as well. After that, there was neither hide nor hair of him out here for many, many years." Moses took a sip of his beer then ended with, "At least that was what my grandpappy remembered and told me."

I ordered another round for the table but Moses waved his off.

"Banks and foreclosures, as popular then as they are now," I mused.

"Nothing changes." Moses nodded.

"So when your grandpappy knew him, when this Armando was riding the train, when did you that occurred?" Rochelle asked.

"Well, like I said," Moses continued, "he became somewhat familiar with my gramps around the turn of the century, after the earthquake ripped up the tracks and had to be rebuilt. So I say, around 1908, that was when the railroad was really running, eventually getting all the way down to Half Moon Bay. But he would never go that far, the Injun that is. My grandpappy said the Injun was definitely tied to this area. The Injun would often hitch a ride from here to just over the hill to what's now the Linda Mar area. And sometimes would just hang out at a station all day, where he would tell tourists how it was to be living as an Injun."

"A life he never really lived, growing up in the Mission, from what I can tell." I added.

"Yesum, lot of things were different back then." Moses said, "Racism prevalent throughout the country. I can't for sure say one group was more discriminated against than another, but if you had Injun blood in you out here, many folks didn't take to kindly toward you. We still had Injun wars in California up through the turn of the century."

Moses paused for a moment, looking into our eyes, apparently checking to see if we were offended by what he had said. We weren't, so he continued. "Anyways, this had been going on for a few years and then before he disappeared for the last time, before the railroad went broke, this Injun told my grandpappy that he had a great treasure hidden in the big mountain out yonder. Said since he was old, it had been harder and harder for him to get to it and he hadn't been able to get to it now none for quite some time. Said he was going to try to get to it one last time but if he couldn't, he would just give my grandpappy a map to the treasure he had hidden as well, and my grandpappy would have to get it on his own. Said since my grandpappy was the only one left who had treated him with respect, he was going to give him that map so my grandpappy would no longer have to work for others."

Moses sat back in his chair and stretched then looked to us for our reactions. I started first.

"I heard it was an engineer who was told about the gold," I said.

"That's probably a throwback to racism," Rochelle quickly interjected. Her eyes were wide with excitement and she was talking fast. "Attributing a white man, and a man with some power, an engineer, to knowing such a secret, I see it all the time. What I find interesting," Rochelle said as she leaned close to Moses, "is the part about a map. That's the first confirmation there actually was a map."

"Oh yesum," Moses said. "There certainly was a map. And he had told my grandpappy generally where he'd have to look in order to find it if he didn't come back."

"Where? Where is it?" Rochelle had her face now so close to Moses that he had to lean back and turn away in his chair. He then reached for his drink and allowed Rochelle to regain her composure and to sit back in her own chair.

71

"Oh, I really can't say." Moses scratched his head, seemingly unnerved. "Can't remember. I meant to say my grandpappy never really mentioned to me exactly where it was and anyways, it wouldn't be right. Not right for the Injun's memory, or my grandpappy's memory. And besides, I think that maybe that the treasure is cursed. It never did the Injun no good. No, I would rather think that things from the past are best left to the past."

"So I take it," I interjected, "after that day, whenever it was, the last day he spoke with your grandpappy, he was never seen again? He never made it back to your grandpappy?"

"Naw, never seen again, as far as I know." Moses sat up in his chair. "You gotta know, Pacifica didn't become a city until 1957. Back in the twenties, that area where the Injun was suppose to be going, was literally a place of hoodlums, a wicked place filled with wicked people. Criminals from San Francisco would hide out there, murderers and others of the most wretched sort. And of course there was the liquor smuggling and prostitution going on. No, I think if the Injun went out there that day he left my grandpappy, some miscreant took advantage of him. Probably killed him and left him out there somewhere. That's what I think happened to him. That's why he never was seen nor heard of again."

I ordered another Budweiser for Moses and extended my hand. "Well Moses," I said, "thanks for your time. It was a pleasure to meet you." I looked to Rochelle and it looked as if her eyes were about to pop out of her head as she shook her head and mouthed the word no.

Moses stood up. I stood up and grabbed Rochelle by the arm and pulled her out of her seat. Moses was nodding with the biggest smile on his face. "So nice to have met you," he said as he shook my hand, "and you as well, darling," he said as he shook Rochelle's hand.

Outside of the Vallamar Station restaurant, Rochelle proceeded to give me a tear down with venom in her voice. "What's wrong with you, Mike?" she spat. "Why the hell did you want to leave? Why didn't we stay to work him?"

"He was done with his story for the day," I replied.

"He was done," Rochelle screamed then pounded her chest, "but I wasn't! Why didn't we get him drunk to get more information out of him? He obviously knew more then he was telling!"

"Calm down," I said putting an arm across her shoulder. "It's all right. Look, he's old and he obviously enjoyed talking with us. And besides, getting him drunk, an innocent—I prefer not to work that way. In time, we can probably get more information out of him, but right now, there wasn't any reason to try to strong arm him. See how he backed off when you were in his face about the map? You blew it right there; he clammed up about the subject."

That did it. Rochelle was in a tailspin. "I blew it? I blew it? You just blew it, mister!" Rochelle shrugged me off her shoulder and jabbed me in the chest with her finger. "You blew it! I don't have all year to coddle some old man, waiting and hoping he'll spill the beans as to where a map might be. We had him right there. We had it!"

Rochelle stomped off to her van and I followed. I tried to grab her by the hand but she shook me away, slammed the door of her van, skidded out of the parking lot and left me to wonder if it was the alcohol, or if this outburst was part of the core of her character.

T HE GATE OF OUR Tenderloin office was closed and I surmised Steve was out and about as I had firmly suggested so I began to circle the Tenderloin and finally found him standing in a doorway out over on Larkin Street, in an area of the Tenderloin that is now called Little Saigon. Steve was looking as if he was talking on his phone. I pulled over, checked my mirrors for any meter maids, and then called his cell. He jumped, startled, then looked at his phone's screen before deciding to take my call.

"Whatcha doing?" I asked.

"I'm on a stakeout," Steve replied.

"What type?" I asked.

"Missing person. Teenager," he said.

"All right. Good. Let's talk," I said. "I'm in the area right now."

"At the office?" Steve asked.

"No," I said. "Right here. I'm actually looking at you."

I watched as Steve looked around. He moved his head like a chicken looking for seeds amid gravel as he looked at all the nearby pedestrians. I decided to give him another news flash. "I'm in my car."

He finally spotted me, smiled and diagonally crossed the street to come to the driver's side window. "Hop on in," I said. We just drove around the block and found a delivery-only spot where we parked with the engine running.

"So what's the story?" I asked.

"A woman came in the other day," Steve began. "She was referred to us from a cop at the station. One of the guys I run into every now and again when I go out and get my morning coffee, told her about us."

"Ahh, that's good news," I replied. "Good, good news. It sounds, then, that we've been acknowledged by the boys."

"Yeah, I see them around," Steve said. "So anyway, this lady, she's out from Nebraska. She's a mom who just wants to talk to her daughter, try to convince her to come home."

"And she knows she's here?" I asked.

"Yeah, from Facebook." Steve said, "Found out from one of the kid's Facebook friends that she is sharing a room with a couple of other girls."

"Working the usual, I suppose."

"Yeah, I think so," Steve said. "I'm checking it. I talked to a couple of hawks who told me there was some fresh meat on the street."

Steve reached into his coat pocket and handed me a picture. The woman in the picture looked like a nice young innocent girl; blue eyes, long hair, freckles. *Poor thing,* I thought to myself. *She won't last long out here.*

"What's her name? I asked.

"Susan. Susan Lakes," Steve replied.

"You need any support?"

"Naw," Steve replied, "I want to try it on my own."

"Good," I said. "But don't hesitate if you get into a jam or need some support. Oh by the way, you talk to Ozzie lately?"

"Yeah, met up with him the other day," Steve replied. "He's good, still a little naïve though."

"Reminds me of another kid I used to know," I said and smiled back at Steve. I turned my car into traffic and drove Steve back to the block from where I had picked him up and gave him some parting advice as he left my car. "Remember to always keep your phone on and charged."

He responded by giving me a British salute.

WEEK III

10

I T WAS EARLY WEDNESDAY morning when my cat Poseidon woke me from a deep sleep. He had somehow made his way under my covers during the night and found a cozy spot to lay his head; his front paws were massaging my face, and the little pricks from his nails had awoken me. I opened my eyes and found his head on one of my pillows. His eyes were closed and he was purring. This time, I had him nailed. It was just a matter of checking my office PC and seeing what the different surveillance cameras I had set up in and outside my bedroom caught through the night. I rolled out of bed and pulled Poseidon from his nirvana just as my phone began to ring.

It was Rochelle on the other end of the line. The weekend had come and gone, as did the first couple of days in the week, with no word from Rochelle and that had made me a little cranky. I was still trying to figure her out, but one thing I knew for sure, I didn't like the way she talked to me, screamed at me, at the end of our last meeting.

"I want you come with me to meet someone, a friend of mine," Rochelle said very dryly.

"Who?" I asked as I threw Poseidon out of the room.

"A friend," she said, still emotionless.

"This isn't the same friend who helps to outfit you is it?" I guessed.

"The one and the same," she said. "He wants to meet you, out over at the Tonga Room. You know where that is?"

"Of course," I said, "up on Cathedral Hill, at the Fairmount, California street side." I waited for a response but Rochelle didn't say anything. "While we're in the City," I said, "do you mind if we swing by Mission Dolores? I want to see if we can find anything out about Amado."

"Sure. Of course," Rochelle said.

"I think it is the oldest spot in San Francisco," I said, "And I've yet to be there. Rochelle," I said, but was greeted with silence. "Rochelle," I repeated and again received only silence. "Rich!" I said.

"Yes," Rochelle said.

"You okay?" I asked as I dressed into a robe.

"Yes," she said. "Just something on my mind."

"Is it about last week and Moses?" I asked. "Care to talk about it?"

"No. Not right now." She said then asked, "Can I pick you up sometime this afternoon?"

I checked my watch. It was seven-thirty in the morning. "Sure," I said. "Around one? At my office?"

"One," she said. "See you then."

I walked through my upstairs bathroom to enter my home office and sat down at my computer desk as Poseidon hopped onto my lap. "Okay, let's see what you've been up to," I said as I tapped the keys on my laptop with my right hand and petted Poseidon with my left.

I fast forwarded through the digital images my cameras had caught throughout the night until I came across the break-in that occurred just after two in the morning. It was Poseidon. The sequential images showed Poseidon coming out of my home office and sitting outside of my bedroom, looking up at the door handle. The door handle was the lever type. Poseidon made a jump and with both front paws on the dropping handle, the door opened. Once inside the bedroom, Poseidon made two circles, and with his second circle, his rump touched the corner of the door and closed it.

"That's it. Busted!" I said, lifting Poseidon off my lap and looking into his face. His response was to purr louder.

I dressed and then headed over to our Pacifica office. I wanted to catch Joe before his morning stroll on over to Cheers.

"Came across something the other day you might be interested in," Joe said as he rocked in his office chair. "I was rereading some of the old papers at the library the other day about the gold rush and trying to see if I could dig up anything about Armando and sure enough, I came across a mention of him in relation to Emperor Norton."

"Emperor Norton?" I asked.

"You never heard of Emperor Norton?" Joe asked.

I said no and Joe shook his head. "Emperor Norton was a Limey who immigrated to San Francisco just after the gold rush. Tried to start a business with some inheritance and the business failed. He then tried to recoup some of it through the courts, lost the rest of his money and basically went nuts for a time, disappearing from the City. When he did finally return, he basically claimed he was Emperor of the United States. Back then, the papers were scandalous and looking for headlines. It seems like there were competitions to see who could come up with the most outlandish things to sell papers, and well, this Norton filled the bill. He began to issue well-written and flamboyant proclamations, such as Congress should be disbanded, and he received a bunch of local support."

"Sounds as if they had issues with Congress back then, just as we do now," I commented.

"And get this," Joe said. "He issued his own money, homemade bank notes that were accepted as local currency. Sound vaguely familiar?"

I nodded. "As in our native friend making his own gold coins?"

"Exactly." Joe said. "Though Emperor Norton was a star of his time. Even the brass at the Presidio gave him an elaborate uniform and the board of supervisors bought him a suit."

Joe passed me a photo he had printed off the microfiche machine from the library. It was picture of Emperor Norton. He had a thick goatee and a uniform, complete with epaulets, plumed hat, sword and dagger on his belt. He did look regal in a way, like a general of the time.

"He died, in front of Old Saint Mary's church out on California Street. Apparently a heart attack. There was huge parade through the city and in one account that I read in the Morning Call, he was attended to by one of his trusted native friends, Armando, who wept at his gravesite for a week."

"That was the only mention of him?" I asked.

"Well, no," Joe said. "Since he was mentioned in the Call, I decided to check that paper more thoroughly and I found several more entries about a native servant often by his side. Doesn't give a name in the other accounts, but I'm guessing it's our guy. Dates I found in the papers were late 1858 through the mid-sixties, though there was very little about him during 1861-1865. The papers are mostly reporting upon the American Civil War during that period. And then there was absolutely no mention of him until January of 1880 when Emperor Norton died. I printed everything I found. It's on your desk."

I listed the dates 1858-1865, 1880 down in my notebook and added the mark 'SF' next to them.

"Help any?" Joe asked.

"Falling into place," I said, "Still tracking him." I added the dates now in the timeline I was developing for Amado's life. "Sounds like when he wasn't in Pacifica, he was in the city, maybe with his friend Emperor Norton. Still have some big gaps. Getting there, though. I'm heading over to Mission Dolores later this afternoon with Rochelle. Maybe I'll be able to fill in some more gaps."

"At the very least," Joe said, "you might be able to get insight into his mindset. Mission Dolores is pretty interesting—well hell, all the missions are pretty interesting to visit but to see where this city sprang up from, to see the roots of a place, that just about beats all hands. And oh, when you're visiting the cemetery, don't forget to pay your respects when you find the gravestone of Carlotta Valdes."

"Who's Carlotta Valdes?" I asked.

"I'll fill you in later," Joe said as he climbed out of his chair with a big grin. "You 'bout ready for a morning pick-me-up?"

"Sure," I said then added, "oh hey, do you have any extra round door handles laying around?"

11

ROCHELLE HAD BEEN PROMPT, right on time. She pulled straight up to our Linda Mar office door but didn't get out. She was strangely quiet and jumpy, and I got the feeling that she was anxious about this meeting, so I pretended to listen to the music on her radio between the times I gave her directions down Highway One to the Two-Eighty freeway and finally to the palm tree lined Dolores Street. We found parking at the corner of Camp and Albion streets, right next to an eye-level plaque that noted at this spot the first chapel of Mission Dolores was built on the edge of a lake that has long since disappeared.

From where we parked, it was just a few short blocks up 16th to Dolores Street and the complex made up of the Basilica Parish of Mission Dolores; the Misión San Francisco de Asís (Mission Dolores), the souvenir shop, museum and graveyard of the old Mission, and across the street, the rectory and various other church owned buildings and residences.

The Basilica, with its grand single and three tiered green copper domed steeples and grossly sculptured and ornate tan colored facade, fails to tower over its squat and unadorned white-washed old Mission Dolores neighbor that has held its ground against what man or nature has thrown at it, surviving both the development of the area from open fields to a city and at least fourteen major earthquakes that had hit the area prior to the 1906 earthquake and subsequent sizable quakes that rolled through the area afterwards, including the 1989 Loma Prieta earthquake.

We climbed the brick stairs and tried to enter the old adobe Mission but the door was closed. A sign read Mass was currently in progress, so we stepped away and noticed an open door with a half gate that looked like it might be a side entrance to the Mission. As it turned out, it was the entrance to the gift shop. We decided to head in but were immediately accosted by a trio of elderly Filipino women who met us at the half gate.

"You wish to enter and take a self guided tour?" asked the closest one to the gate.

"Yes, we would," I replied.

"Then a small donation is requested," the woman replied. She was wearing a black shawl over her head and her name badge stated her name was Lourdes. The other two women nodded in agreement and I coughed up the ten dollar donation fee to get both Rochelle and myself into the Mission.

"Here you are," Lourdes said as she handed us just one self guided tour brochure as we entered. "Since mass has started," she continued as she pointed with a shaky finger, "may I suggest you run the tour in reverse, starting in the graveyard via the back door of the gift shop?"

"Thank you. We will," I said, glancing down at the brochure as I walked around the gift shop, looking for the book section. Rochelle was already heading for the back of the gift shop and the back door when Lourdes asked me if I had been there before.

"Can't say that I have," I replied.

Lourdes smiled and her associates sidled up to her. "Where are you from?" asked one whose name badge read Maria.

"Born and raised in the city, but I now live in Pacifica," I replied.

"Oh, my sister lived out there for a time. Very beautiful," said the woman whose badge stated her name was Grace.

"Yes," I agreed, then to extricate myself, "mind if we look around?"

"Oh yes," Lourdes said, "please do." The three women went back to talking amongst themselves about how beautiful the day was turning out to be when another elderly woman wandered in wearing a bright flower print scarf, a black overcoat and handbag. I found the book section but couldn't help overhearing their conversation as I perused the available titles. Rochelle was nowhere to be seen.

"Oh, I'm running late. I see they started Mass already," this new woman said as she placed her purse upon the counter.

"Oh," Lourdes said, "who was it for?"

"Madeline," said Maria.

"Really?" Lourdes replied. "I hadn't heard."

"It was last Tuesday," Grace said

"Yes, last Tuesday," added the new woman in black. "During the night she went to meet her maker." They all nodded.

"I was with her in the morning. We had coffee in her sunroom and the next day when I dropped by, she didn't answer so I let myself in."

"She sometimes didn't come to the door," Lourdes said.

"Hard of hearing," Maria added.

"And her eyesight!" Grace shook her head and they all agreed upon how bad Madeline's eyesight had been.

"I found her still in bed, peaceful as could be," said the woman in black.

"I think she was ready," Lourdes said.

"I was born ready," Maria said and again they all agreed.

I marveled at the way they talked. There was no sadness in their friend's departure and they didn't seem upset that they missed the funeral mass for their friend next door. It was as if death of their friend was a minor episode in that person's daily life: *Oh she woke up, got a coffee, went shopping, died, and went to heaven. I think she's feeling pretty good right now.* Their attitude was something I was quite unaccustomed to, having come across so many people who had died and their emotional relations in my line of work. I wondered if it was just their age, or maybe some mysterious religious wisdom they possessed. Maybe if I started to go to church . . . I put the book down I had been glancing through and headed to the back of the gift shop, to where Rochelle had been waiting. We exited the gift shop as had been suggested and entered the graveyard.

"I think I read somewhere that it is the oldest and now only graveyard within the city limits," Rochelle said, moving quickly down the side edge of the graveyard and toward what the map had noted would be the museum entrance. "All of the graveyards were moved to Colma as the city expanded."

I stopped at the first marker and called out, "If you don't count the military graveyard in the Presidio. And the graveyard for Thomas Starr King at the Unitarian Church up on Geary."

Rochelle had walked all the way down the side of the graveyard and then came back. "The museum entrance is down here," she said.

I ignored her comment. "And there are graveyards that never were moved and just had their markers taken away and then were built upon, like the graveyard they found in the 90s when they were doing some remodeling work over at the Palace of Legion of Honor, and if you don't count the pet cemetery underneath the Golden Gate Bridge's Doyle drive—have you ever been there? Nice one, white picket fence . . ."

I could tell I was getting on Rochelle's nerves. She wanted me to move, but I was in absolutely no rush and began to take the circuitous path that wound throughout the cemetery, so she took it too, walking fast ahead of me and barely glancing at the markers. At one point, the path led to a replica of an Ohlone thatched house that was standing amid the tombstones and statues. "Says there are upwards of 5,000 Indians buried in this little graveyard. Unmarked graves, mass graves of the Indians. So sad."

That comment seemed to bring some solemness to Rochelle. She came back to where I was standing and looked at the thatched house. "Nice," she said, then, "come on."

"Oh hey," I said, "keep an eye out for a gravestone with the name Carlotta Valdes."

"Who's she?" Rochelle asked.

"Never mind," I said to conceal my ignorance. "Just know that it is important to find it."

We continued down the path and Rochelle's gait slowed as we walked around the graveyard, reading the names of the departed, or at least I was reading them. Rochelle kept her head down and still seemed to only be glancing at the tombstones and monuments. Something was definitely on her mind, and it obviously wasn't this place.

As we continued down the path, I found myself reading and contemplating every name on every tombstone. So many in such a compact space. Many of the stones bore names that can be found as street names within the city: Arguello, Bernal, de Haro, Moraga, Noe, Sanchez.

Near the end of path in the cemetery is a statue of Father Junipero Serra. I paused and contemplated the man who founded the Franciscan order. "I'm going over to the museum," Rochelle yelled to me as she stood by an archway that led out of the graveyard and to the museum. "Are you coming or are you planning on making some sort of offering?"

I shook off her comment and as I followed her, I asked, "No Carlotta?"

"Nope," she answered.

Surprisingly, the museum itself was more dedicated to lives of the native peoples rather than the missionaries. I guess the building, the mission itself, is a museum for the latter. There were dioramas of the Mission as established, life in the mission, and life in the nearby villages prior to the Spanish arriving. There were displays of native artifacts such as tools used for hunting and baskets. There were displays of their clothing pre—and post—Missionary arrival.

As I toured the museum, Rochelle was by my side, nudging me along and every so often checking her watch. Her prodding succeeded, and I quickly found myself at the museum exit, which led us back to the gift shop.

"Did you enjoy your visit?" Lourdes asked as we returned to the gift shop.

"Yes, we did," I said. "Informative, but I was hoping to find out a little more about how the area over in my town of Pacifica, what is now the Sanchez Adobe, and that supported this mission. As in, would any of the local natives have been brought up from the Pacifica area?"

"Oh, yes, of course." Lourdes said. "Besides being a place where they grew and raised food in support of the Mission, the records showed that many of the natives from the coast originally came from the village of Puristac, which was by then the San Pedro y San Pablo Asistencia. What is now called the old Sanchez Adobe."

"Ever hear of someone in the history of this place by the name of Amado or Armando?" I asked.

"No, no, can't say I have," Lourdes said. "Though there are countless names listed in the archives. Do you have any more information about him? Something to narrow down the years he may have been at the Mission, where he came from, something along those lines?"

"I think he may have been an Ohlone, from Puristac, but I'm just guessing." I said then checked my notebook as Rochelle checked her watch. "He was here probably here around the 1820s," I said.

Lourdes nodded, bit her lip, and then said, "I have something that might help."

She bent low behind the counter and beneath the shelves of books for sale, she slid open one of the doors on the lower cabinet to reveal a line of large red binders.

"These are copies of the translated version of all of the records of the Mission," Lourdes said as she placed a binder upon the countertop. "Father Emilio allowed us to make copies of the translated versions of books so we could study and learn from them in our Sunday reading circle, though we never went too far into them. The clean versions of these are a set of fine red books that Father Emilio keeps in the rectory for researchers. He also has a straight copy, the untranslated version, in the rectory. The originals that all of these copies were made or translated from are at the Vatican. If you need to look at the untranslated copies, you will need to speak with Father Emilio."

"These copies are fine," I said. "Besides, I don't speak or read Latin or Spanish. May I see the binders from maybe 1820 through 1840?"

"Yes, of course," Lourdes said.

"And mind if we use the table over there?" I asked, pointing to a round table and chairs in the corner.

"Please do," she replied.

Rochelle grudgingly joined me as I made a couple of trips from the counter to the table and then dove into the worn binders. These binders, basically books of the mission, even though translated, took awhile to get used to in their reading. The writing style was very different to what I'm accustomed to reading, but basically they were meticulous calendars of daily events, ceremonies, supplies, and people. Even though these were Xerox copies, I couldn't help but liken them to Mission diaries and couldn't help but feel a bit of reverence as I skimmed through them.

"We should really probably be getting on our way soon," Rochelle said. "We can come back another time." I waved her off and added a 'hold on' or two.

I had gone through the binders, getting used to the layout and reading style, when I finally got the bright idea to place them in year order. I dug out the binder from 1820 and began to skim the pages when I found an entry about a baby being brought to the Mission. "I think I may have found him," I said aloud.

Rochelle came around to look over my shoulder to read. The entry noted the arrival to the Mission of a native woman with a newborn. They apparently were starving and had walked from somewhere along the coast. The woman's name was not mentioned but later entries noted the child was baptized as Armando.

"I need to call my friend," Rochelle finally said, "and tell him we're going to be running a little late." She headed out the back door and into the cemetery. I kept looking through the binders and lost track of time. I guess it was maybe half an hour before Rochelle came back in. "Everything okay?" I asked.

"Yes," she said, "My friend understands. He said it was important research to find all that we could about Armando. Maybe it could help us to locate the go . . ." she slipped, "locate his grave and his life story. He said maybe we could meet him around five at the Tonga room."

"Sure. No problem. Besides," I said, "looks like this place closes at four."

I continued skimming through the binders. Around 1823 I came across an entry that noted the mother of the child Armando was reprimanded for calling her child Amado, Beloved. Apparently she had learned the word and decided to rename her son Amado.

Amado's name came up once or twice as Armando in the binders in the eighteen twenties, then a few times in the thirties. Throughout there were reprimands noted to his mother for calling him Amado, until her passing in 1838. When we entered the forties, the name Armando was scattered about in the binders. We traded in the binders that we had skimmed through for the set that documented life at the Mission in the forties. By 1842, things were more than dire, with less than a dozen Indians living at Mission Dolores. Throughout the forties, the name Armando appeared as he became the man around the Mission: blacksmith, carpenter, mason, artisan, roofer. Then all of a sudden, his name completely disappeared from the binder of 1849. We checked a few later binders and his name did not come up. We went back to the binder of 1848 and came a across a single entry and possibly a final recognition. "Amado . . . gone."

"What do you think happened?" Rochelle asked.

"It doesn't really say. But as you know, in 1848, gold was reported in San Francisco and the gold rush began. Many people disappeared, and it looks like he did, as well. Maybe he was seduced by gold fever to head for the hills."

I turned back to the beginning of the binder and read an entry for January 1848. It simply read, "Gold discovered!"

It was now a quarter to four so we brought the binders to Lourdes and thanked her.

"Since we're here, I just want to take a quick look inside the Mission," I told Rochelle. "Is it okay?" I asked Lourdes.

"Yes," Lourdes said, "there's still time."

"And oh, one more thing," I said. "A friend of mine said to look for Carlotta Valdes' gravestone. I checked but didn't see it. Where is it?"

"You have a funny friend," Lourdes said.

"What?" I asked.

"You ever see Alfred Hitchcock's movie *Vertigo*?" Lourdes asked.

"Long time ago," I said and Rochelle nodded.

"In that movie, the star Kim Novak is shown looking at the gravestone of a dead relative, Carlotta Valdes. That scene was filmed in this graveyard and for many years, there was a gravestone for Carlotta Valdes out there. It was later removed out of respect for those who truly are buried there."

"And rightly so," I said.

"Rightly so," repeated Lourdes.

We thanked Lourdes and her friends, headed out the front door of the gift shop, and entered the Mission church proper. Inside, we found ourselves standing under the choir loft, the original redwood beams above us and leading all the way to the sacristy having been painted in a chevron pattern alternating in orange, red, gray and white. The walls of the church, the same white as found on the walls surrounding the mission, were bathed in a warm light from chandeliers and from sun filtering in from the windows located high above. A mural, several religious statues and paintings that appeared to be in gaudy frames adorned the otherwise bare walls. Rochelle took a step inward, but I had already seen enough, having already seen many previous mission churches. I pulled out my notebook and stepped directly under a chandelier, and updated my timeline.

"Okay, so what I have now is Amado was born around 1820 on the coast, maybe around the area of the Sanchez Adobe, aka San Pablo Asistencia, which was also the location of an Ohlone village called Pruristac," I said, beginning my recap of all of what we had learned of Amado up to that point. "Shortly thereafter, he arrives with his mom at Mission Dolores. Here he is baptized and renamed Armando, and is nicknamed Amado by his mother. He lived and worked at Mission Dolores, doing everything from brick maker and painter to blacksmith. In 1848, the gold rush is on and he disappears, probably into the wilderness to hunt for gold. Then around 1859 he shows up again, in San Francisco, tagging along with Emperor Norton."

"Emperor Norton?" Rochelle asked.

I filled her in with as much as I knew about Emperor Norton from Joe, and continued, "Anyway, apparently while he was in the gold fields, he had made some sort of fortune, enough at least to try to purchase some land, possibly his ancestral land where the Sanchez Adobe was now sitting basically abandoned. Since he was a native, he basically was refused the opportunity and he became a squatter until he was kicked off the land when Bank of America foreclosed on the current owners."

"There is no mention of him that we've found until 1880," I said as I flipped the page of my notebook, "when he is seen for a time in San Francisco again, when his friend Emperor Norton passed away. Then sometime after that, he made his way back down here to the coast, possibly Pacifica. In his later years, it sounds like he basically became homeless, possibly a drunkard, finding a friend in Moses' grandfather and then finally disappearing with the last train at the age of about a hundred."

Rochelle agreed with my summation, then continued with, "So what do you think, Mike? Do you think there is a gold treasure out there?"

I tapped the top of my notebook with my pen. "I could see him not really trusting anyone near the end, racism being so prevalent back then, and his family long gone. If I was in his shoes, I wouldn't want anyone I didn't know or trust to have it, either, except maybe the one guy who gave me some respect."

"Moses' grandfather." Rochelle said.

"Moses' grandfather," I repeated. "But if he ran through it all, or drank it all, or had it all stolen from him before he disappeared, I'm not sure."

The lights inside the church flicked off. They were closing shop. Rochelle and I stepped out of the church, and I paused just outside the doors while Rochelle waited for me on the sidewalk. It was nice outside. There was a break in the clouds that sent sunshine down upon the Mission, and parrots began to squawk from the palm trees planted in the street median. Both Rochelle and I looked but couldn't catch a glimpse of them within the palm fronds.

Late in 1848, Amado had left this mission, maybe stood where I was now standing, and decided to head east toward the gold fields, where he struck it rich. He then, for the rest of his life, wandered back and forth between the City and what would eventually become Pacifica. In the end, he disappeared and I daydreamed that possibly, hopefully, he died peacefully, meeting his maker somewhere near his ancestral grounds in what once was the village of Pruristac.

12

FROM MISSION DOLORES, I guided Rochelle to Cathedral Hill and toward the Tonga Room, where at times as we drove, we could hear the contents of her van shift either toward the front or back of the van, depending on whether we were climbing or descending one of the steep hills. We finally found parking in a garage and trudged the half block of California to the main entrance of the Tonga Room inside of the Fairmont Hotel.

The Tonga Room and Hurricane Bar is one of the original Tiki themed restaurants and bars that serves Pacific Rim cuisine, along with tropical fruit-filled drinks that arrive in tall thin glasses with little umbrellas or in opened coconuts that have straws as long as a man's arm. In this bamboo and plastic tropical setting, thatched roof booths line the sides of the restaurant, while wicker chairs and rough hewn tables dot the interior space that resembles a fishing dock. Plastic palm trees, fishing nets with colorful glass floaters, wooden barrels and boxes and ship lights adorn pier pilings and the thick rope railing that keeps patrons from falling into an encircled artificial lake that takes up the middle of the restaurant. Occasionally, and to the accompaniment of thunder, there is a downpour within this restaurant as sprinklers spring to life from the restaurant's ceiling and create a downpour of 'rain' that falls into the lake.

"There he is!" Rochelle said excitedly, pushing me from behind toward a row of tables that lined the left side of the artificial lake.

Midway down this row of tables, underneath a plastic palm tree, sat a white haired man with a neatly trimmed goatee. He's one of those type of guys who at first glance looks overweight but fit. He was wearing white slacks and a Tommy Bahama shirt. His white dinner jacket was slung over the back of his chair. He was at least four hundred and fifty pounds and maybe a shade more, although it was hard to tell for sure as he sat with his body pouring off his chair on all sides like a human landslide. As we approached, he slowly stood, using his table for support. When we met, his hand pressed mine equally as hard, which surprised me since I was guessing his pillow-sized hands would be soft.

"Colin Broadmore," the fat man juicily said.

"Mike Mason," I replied.

"So Rich has been telling me a lot about you," he breathed heavily. His voice was deep and there was a gurgling sound that accompanied his voice when he spoke. "Here, join me," he said as he dropped back into his chair, as if his legs were no longer able to support him. His wicker chair screamed at his weight and he nearly knocked over his wine and empty bread basket as he rocked the small wooden table between us. "Rich, please be so kind as to give us a few moments alone," Colin said, "and make sure the waitress knows we are to be left alone unless she is called upon."

Colin took a breath, and I thought he'd suck all the air out of the room.

Rochelle looked at me, a bit shaken, then hastily nodded and headed back to the Hurricane Bar. I turned in my chair to watch her. She spoke to a waitress, pointed to where we were sitting and slipped something into her hand. The waitress checked what was given her, nodded, looked to us then back to Rochelle, before nodding and continuing on with her job.

"So Rich tells me you've been extremely helpful in what is becoming my current pet project, this search for Armando's Gold," Colin said, bringing my attention back to him.

"Amado." I said.

"What?" The folds of Colin's brow avalanched over his eyebrows.

"I believe the man's name, the one he was probably most comfortable with, was Amado," I said.

Colin waved my answer off as if it was an annoying fly. "Whatever." He continued as his brow reflexed back into an accordion, "The name is not what is important but what I do find important is this friend of yours."

"Friend of mine?" I asked.

"This friend of yours," Colin continued, "the one who found this bit of gold. Can you trust him?" Colin took a deep breath, the bellows of his lungs incessantly working. "Might he be the type that, might I say, be holding out on you on what he knows, or what he has?"

Before I had a chance to answer, Colin interrupted me by lifting his empty bread basket into the air and flagging down the waitress, and a gurgling sound erupted from deep inside him like a sputtering mud-pot. "Waitress, more bread please!" I noted to myself he hadn't waiting to long before asking to be interrupted by a waitress.

"Yes," I said as Colin's hungry eyes followed the waitress to a side table near the front of the restaurant and then back to us. "I've known him for most of my life." I continued, "And I can firmly say he is telling me everything."

The waitress exchanged our empty bread basket with what I guess was the other half of a loaf already consumed at this table. Colin greedily grabbed at the bread that looked no more than the size of a regular bun in his enormous hands. He tore two slices off the half loaf, opened a square pat of cold butter, tried smearing it onto the bread with its gold wrapper, then resorted to just pressing the butter into the bread with one of his giant thumbs. He then grabbed two more pats and did the same, sucked in the spittle that was forming around the edges of his mouth in anticipation, and then sat back in his chair alternating between chewing and breathing. He looked around the restaurant as he chewed, then midway through his second slice of bread he sat up, took a gigantic swallow of wine, smacked his lips to sufficiently clear his mouth and said, "Mr. Mason, when I'm after something, I will stop at nothing to get it. Nothing will get in my way. Rich can vouch for that."

Having watched him eat the bread, all I could do was agree by nodding my head.

"I have some unpleasant matters I need to attend to. Nothing to do with this current project that you are working on with Rich, but another one that has been nagging me for quite sometime that I wish to wrap up. You, Mr. Mason, your particular skills, I believe can be of some service to me."

"I'm open to all entreaties," I said.

"You're in the detective business, Rich tells me." He coughed.

"Yes, yes I am."

"Well, I'm sure being in the business that you are, you sometimes see things shall I say, a little differently than the average Joe."

I watched Colin's eyes move from me to over my shoulder and toward the Hurricane Bar. I turned in my seat and could see Rochelle leaning against the bar, a drink in her hand, watching us. I caught Colin pointing to her, making a little swirling movement with one of his pudgy fingers and Rochelle responded, dropping her head as if she was caught by the principal, then turned away to have her back to us.

Colin snorted and I turned completely to face him again. My face flushed. I didn't like how he seemed to own her. How he ordered her around. It irked me a bit.

"I like to keep my eyes open." I returned to our conversation.

"That's good. Very good," Colin replied. "You see, I have a certain situation, a project that just isn't going the way I expected it to go, and I now need a good man to finish it, to take care of this project to the very end, so to speak."

"And the cost?" I asked. "What do I get out of it?"

"You will be compensated handsomely," Colin said. "But beware, I demand the utmost professionalism on your part. No slip-ups."

I leaned back into my chair and it crackled uncomfortably, and I decided to just lay it out on the table. "So this situation, I take it that you are talking about," I said, "is in the two-legged form and you want me to dispose of him or her."

Colin nodded.

I leaned forward and onto the table, as close to Colin as I could get. "Are you serious?" I asked.

"Mr. Mason," Colin replied, "not only I am serious, I am dead serious."

I looked at him squarely into his eyes. "Fuck off," I said.

"Excuse me?" Colin coughed.

"I said, fuck off!" I repeated

Colin began to laugh, his whole body shaking like an erupting volcano as his chair squirmed.

I sat back, watched him for a few moments then looked toward the artificial lake, disgusted with the man.

"Mr. Mason, you are not the type of man that minces words, are you?" Colin finally said as he dappled saliva from the corners of his mouth. "I like that. Rich said you were a straight shooter. And I was just testing you. I like that. I like to know who I'm dealing with."

"Glad you like it," I said dryly. "Now what is it that you really want?"

"What I want, what I want." Colin pondered the question. He then swiveled in his chair and reached inside his jacket pocket to retrieve a legal-sized security envelope. He looked at the front of the envelope, turned it over and placed it on the table in front of me.

I flipped the envelope over and found my name was written on it in black pen in a very curvy and exaggerated script.

"What's this?" I asked feeling the envelope's weight and deducing it did not contain any bills.

"From my employer." Colin said and turned a hand over to say open it and find out.

I flicked the envelope back across the table. I was getting tired of his games. "You open it."

I watched as one of Colin's thick fingers got nicked as he struggled to open the envelope. "Ouch!" he said then slurped the drop of blood that formed on his finger. He then pulled a single piece of paper from inside the envelope and scanned it quickly to get a general gist of it. When he was done, he smirked and coughed out a laugh.

"What's so funny?" I asked.

"Nothing, nothing," Colin said, then, "and I thought Rich had brought you to me but it seems that my employer had his eye on you long before Rich stumbled upon your acquaintance."

I furrowed my brow in response.

"Seems my employer wished for you to know something though this letter," Colin continued, "but since you refused, let me try to convey the general contents of this letter to you. Let's see." Colin looked over the letter again. "Seems you have come to his attention for some reason. Let me see if I can find it. Hmm, it starts off with a bit of your history: born January 15, 1969 to Anna and Frank Mason. At age eight, you ran away from home, were sent to a military school and ran away from that. Your juvenile record, hmm, impressive. Let's see, what else—oh, you came under the care of Joe Ballard of Ballard and Son, later to be called Coastside Detectives. Let's see, what else? Hmm, some quite interesting tidbits here, and oh, some questionable activities. Ahh, Mr. Mason, well I would never have guessed you went to prison for a spell, to '. . . *protect a client's confidentiality.*' Really, Mr. Mason. You really are a man of character. Hmm, let's see, what else? Oh this is interesting. You seem not to be one to be trifled with, '. . . *having been connected to the deaths of at least fifteen people over the years*', and not to mention the deaths that can be attributed to your '. . . *involvement in the partial breakup of a West Coast smuggling ring.*' Really, Mr. Mason," Colin said, "I had no idea."

"Give it here!" I said as I snatched the letter from Colin's hand.

The same exaggerated script that was on the front of the envelope was on the letter. I quickly read it and found it to be basically a short biography of me. When I was through, I carefully folded up the letter and placed it into my pocket.

"So you and, 'your employer' have my life story," I said. "Nowadays, anyone's life can come under scrutiny and to light. Just need someone who is good with a computer and just about anything or everything can be found out about someone. Take you, for example. I can have one of my partners do the same about you and the next time I'll invite you to lunch and I can hand you an envelope."

Colin laughed a big sloppy spittle-filled laugh.

"You need to begin talking straight with me and telling me what this is all about," I said, "otherwise I'm getting out of here."

"Calm down now, Mr. Mason." Colin tried to lean forward, but his girth disallowed any movement across the table. "Beyond what plans my employer wishes to make with you, the real reason I wanted to meet you was Rich."

I looked over my shoulder. Rochelle had her back to us and appeared to be talking up the bartender.

"Rich tends to be a little on the imaginative side," Colin said, "She needs someone stable to direct her. Her innovative approaches, fanciful leaps and intuitive thinking have brought me as well as my employer good fortune, Mr. Mason, and I consider her to be the daughter—rather, the child—that I never had, but that being said, she is a child. She acts like one and likes to spend my money recklessly. I need someone to keep tabs on her. Someone who can rein her in. Keep her from gallivanting about recklessly with our money."

I was still a little ticked at having someone looking into my past without my knowing, but now I was getting pissed again at how he seemed to perceive Rochelle. "Look, I'm not your baby sitter," I said. "I'm not into games. I'm not your assassin. And I'm just about done with all of these shenanigans."

I must have raised my voice pretty loud for I watched Colin's eyes look in the direction where I last saw Rochelle. Again, I turned my head to see her. She was now facing us, resting her elbows and leaning her back onto the Hurricane Bar; in her hands she held what appeared to be a Pina Colada. She raised her drink as if to make a toast to us and, I responded by turning to face Colin. It was irking me that she was being led by someone I considered disgusting and an ass.

Again, a look of disdain must have been on my face, for Colin let out another slobbering and snorting laugh just as the sound of electronic thunder bellowed into the room and was followed by water falling into the artificial lake.

"This rain shower," Colin said. "It reminds me of a place Rich and I once traveled."

He emptied the contents of the bottle of wine into his glass, then raised the empty bottle to signal a waitress to bring another.

"Do you know anything about Haiti, Mr. Mason?" Colin asked after taking a swig that emptied half his glass of wine.

"I know I don't ever want to go there," I said, "especially since the earthquake."

"Precisely," Colin said. "Yet it is places such as Haiti, places that most people shun, that can often be the most profitable. Let me illustrate this in a little story."

Colin paused as the waitress arrived with another bottle of wine, took the empty and received an order from Colin for a Tonga Platter.

"I once had a dog, Mr. Mason, a fine dog, a German Shepard," Colin continued. "This dog was the most unusual dog that I ever had in that he liked blackberries—you know, the type of berries that grows in thorny brambles? Well, this dog loved them. He would seek out the choicest berries and what he would do, was to line up with his target and in the slowest and most cautious of movements, he would step into the brambles, even closing his eyes as he pushed his head into the brambles surrounded by thorny barbs, gently picking the berry, and slowly retrace his steps out of the bush, never once getting pricked by the thorns." Colin stopped as the waitress returned with the Tonga Platter.

The Tonga Platter turned out to be a tray filled with pork ribs, coconut prawns, spring rolls and chicken satay. It was enough for two, though I wasn't eating and I don't believe Colin ever made the offer. He grabbed a couple of pork ribs, his fingers becoming sloppy red with barbeque and pork fat juices. He slurped on his fingers as he pulled every last bit of flesh from the bones.

Watching him eat was making my stomach turn. "There was a book I read when I was a kid," I said, "about a kid picking blueberries. As he filled his pail, a baby bear ate from his pail until it was almost empty. The book was called 'Blueberries for Sal'. I don't get what you're driving at."

Colin nodded in his own childhood reminiscence as he retrieved a bone from deep inside his mouth and then continued, "That's how I like to operate Mr. Mason."

"You like stealing other people's berries," I said, "or in your story, picking berries amid thorns?"

"I like to take my time," Colin said. "Sometimes matters are delicate. Sometimes you must carefully maneuver yourself among the brambles to get to the prize. Be cautious and you will reap your rewards. With Rich . . . sometimes with Rich, she just can't do that. She gets too excited. She becomes clumsy and in my line of work, that can have some financially dire consequences for me, my financiers, and employer. So in that respect, I see that I simply can no longer afford the luxury of keeping her under such loose reins. I need someone who can be with her at all times, placate those, when the need arises, and not just instantly respond aggressively to every situation."

"I said I was no nursemaid."

"And I heard you," Colin agreed. He poured himself more wine just as another faux rain shower began. "Ah," Colin paused as he glanced over his shoulder to watch the sprinklers create their magic, "back to the rain and Haiti."

Colin adjusted himself in his chair, his chair creaking under his mass, then continued. "My employer at the time, the one who has such interests in you," Colin motioned with a fat finger toward the envelope I had in my pocket, "had come upon some details about an early Spanish mine that was again ready to be actively exploited. The potential of this mine yielding some immense profits was nearly unimaginable, but to get it would require political finesse at very deep local and governmental levels."

"And money, no doubt." I said.

"Bribery, yes, or what I rather call, assurances. The thing is, Mr. Mason, these assurances weren't distributed the way they should have been, as I had planned and well, feathers were ruffled, some rather reckless things were said and done and needless to say, with several individuals now just ghosts of their former selves and the earthquake destroying the little infrastructure they previously had, I dare not attempt to try to recoup our losses directly from that country."

"Must have hurt some to invest so much and to, I'm guessing, run away with nothing to show for it."

"Precisely, it was indeed a great financial loss," Colin nodded, "However the loss was felt mostly by my employer. That, along with some other pressures he has been feeling of late, some of which I'm beginning to believe may have been by your hand, and I find myself in a hole, scrambling to make payments back up the food chain faster than I could have ever imagined."

"Well, things are tough all over." I said as I stared directly at Colin. "And I can't say I'm feeling too sorry for you or for any of your associates, be they your employer or your partners." I rolled my eyes back toward Rochelle. I was getting a whole new picture of her.

Colin snorted a laugh. "Mr. Mason," Colin said, "let me be straight with you. Rich has a nose for gold and when she catches a whiff of it, there is no stopping her. And here, here we have come to the conclusion there is gold. Gold is here, Mr. Mason. Nearby. Possibly lots of it. And it is easy pickings. That first coin that was found was merely a single berry on a larger bush that is just waiting to be plucked clean."

"Well, you're the man with the need and if it is that easy, I still don't see why you need me. Even if Rich is as reckless as you claim, in this case, as far as I've seen, it is just a matter of finding it, or digging it up."

"Have you every picked berries, Mr. Mason?"

"Oh God," I said, "not another analogy."

"I take it that you haven't," Colin said, ignoring my comment. "Well, if you had, you would have learned that no matter how careful you were, even if the berries were right there within your grasp, you would doubtless come away from your venture with your fingertips stained. I do not wish to get my fingers stained however I propose to you Mr. Mason, that you join us on this venture, directly, and I think it will go a long way in paying back the debt you owe."

"I don't owe anybody anything." I said.

"Oh don't be so sure of yourself," Colin countered. "My employer's hand is far reaching. Perhaps from that letter you have in your pocket, you can glean some clues as to where your paths may have crossed and where you had made some offense. Regardless, my employer is not the sort of man who would normally be so kind as to offer you such a carrot. I see that letter you have as a peace offering and an invitation. An invitation for you to make amends, no doubt. That is why you are here, Mr. Mason, and still walking this earth. It is so you can take your first step in making your own personal restitution to my employer, and together with me, Rich and her husband . . ."

"Her what?" I interrupted Colin.

"Her husband." Colin burped and hit his chest.

The color of my face must have changed, for Colin started laughing. "Oh, did Rich forget to tell you? Did *I* forget to tell you we had another partner, Rich's husband? Did she forget to tell you she was married?"

That was it. Colin's laughter fell upon my ears and rang like church bells. I tried to shut him out by clamping my hands over my ears, but it didn't help. His laughter was loud, penetrating, and I felt sick. Sick and mad. I got up and knocked over the table Colin and I were sitting at; the food, drinks and dishes crashed to the floor. Colin remained sitting; the initial look of shock on his face was quickly replaced with even more laughter.

"You think that's funny, fat boy?" I yelled. "You think that's funny?" I picked up the table, put it on my shoulder and then heaved it into the lake.

Colin's laughter grew even louder as he rocked in his chair, slapping his legs. Patrons throughout the restaurant were pointing, getting out of their chairs, gasping or muttering things within their parties. I looked behind me, and I could hear the bartender back by Rich screaming something in Tagalog on the telephone. I headed for the door with Colin calling out between fits of laugher, "Don't go. Please stay. We have so much more to talk about."

As I neared the bar and the exit, the waitress, joined by the bartender, tried to stop me, but I pushed them aside. I glared at Rich as I passed her. Her eyes were wide and her mouth open.

"Hey!" Rich called out as I left the room. "Hey!"

But I wasn't stopping. I knocked open the Tonga Room's glass doors, headed down the hall and out of the Fairmont to jump out onto the California Street sidewalk. A cable car happened to be rumbling down the street, and I ran out and caught the tail end of it and swung aboard. I looked back as Rich exited the Tonga Room, looked down at me on the cable car and gave me a wave. I turned away, looked down California Street and counted the straight blocks to the approaching end of the cable car line; too many blocks to go. I needed more distance fast and needed to not have the feeling that Rich was watching the cable car and me all the way to the end of the line. I hopped off the cable car at Grant Street and followed Grant through the Chinatown gate and through Union Square. I then got the idea to continue on over to our Tenderloin branch as it was only a few blocks away. I needed air, I needed time to think, I needed a walk and needed to get my mind off Rich.

13

T HE WALK FROM WHERE I had hopped off the cable car to our Tenderloin office turns out, did me amazingly good. As I got closer to the office, I felt my spirits lift and my mood lighten as I began to slip into my work mode and anticipated catching up with Steve and seeing his progress on his case, as well as seeing the shape of the office. Indeed, the brisk walk was doing me such wonders, as soon as I turned the corner from Jones onto Eddy, it seemed that even the very sidewalk in front of our place was cleaner and brighter.

"There's a sidewalk cleaner that comes by every other week," Steve said when I asked him if I was just seeing things about the overall cleanliness of the space in front of our building. "He rides what looks like a mini street sweeper that cleans the sidewalks. I threw him an extra ten spot to make a couple of extra passes in front of the shop."

I nodded my approval. I then ran a finger across one of the metal steam heaters and my finger became caked with dust.

"The insides still looks like hell." I said as I eyed open cabinets and folders.

"Working on it." Steve said.

Then I heard the toilet flush and the sink water turn on and off. I pointed to the bathroom, hoping it was a client, and Steve only had a chance to nod before the door opened wide to reveal a young heavyset black woman wearing a loosely hanging red blouse. As she exited the lavatory, she stuffed her blouse into her faded tight blue jeans.

"Oh Lordy, don't go walking in there!" the woman said fanning the air behind her. "That's the last time I go to Sloppy's!" She then noticed that I had entered the office.

"Well, hey!" the woman said tilting her head with the biggest and sweetest smile she could muster. "Welcome to the offices of Coastside Detectives."

"Hi," I replied somewhat befuddled.

Steve quickly stood up. "Ah Mike, this is Marilyn. Marilyn, this is Mike, Mike Mason, one of my partners . . . he's *my* boss."

Marilyn sashayed up to me in response, all lips and lipstick, five three and three hundred pounds. She then gave me a hand in a very business-like manner. "So nice to meet you . . . honey."

"She's my intern," Steve said.

"An intern." I was shocked. "We already have an intern. *You* already have an intern, Ozzie. You can barely keep track of him!"

"I know, I know," Steve said. "But Marilyn is really good. She knows her stuff."

"No offense to you," I said to Marilyn, "but we really cannot handle another body."

"Mike, just listen," Steve said. "I know what you're thinking, that having another person is too much to handle, but it's not. It is just the opposite."

"I'll just let you two talk this out," Marilyn interjected as she headed for a chair across the room. I watched her, and I swear, if someone was walking beside her, the swish of her hips would have knocked them to the floor. I shook my head and continued with Steve.

"Steve, you can't go making these types of business decisions without speaking first with Joe or myself," I said.

"I know, I know. Maybe I jumped the gun," Steve countered. "But you said I needed to make our presence known out here and I am, but in doing that, I just don't have the time to do anything else. I have all of these files to sort through, I have Ozzie to teach, you still want me to run the office, invoicing and accounting. I need someone out here who is skilled in office work, is capable of doing that and has knowledge and interest in the area, and Marilyn has both!"

"And we're going to crack the murder of your other partner's father," Marilyn interjected.

Steve turned red. "We're just going over the old cases. Learning about them. Talking about them between us, to see what we could learn."

Marilyn climbed out of her chair and again swished her way over to me. "Mr. Mason, I'm fully qualified. I got a degree from Phoenix University and I put myself through school. I can type sixty-five words a minute, do the accounting for my father *and* was born and raised in the area. What more could you ask for? And I bet I can get into places you'll never be able to get into. Look, Mr. Mason, I'm not asking for money yet; I just want to get my feet wet and help the people out in the neighborhood. As soon as I heard my daddy mention you folks in one of his sermons the other day, and how you helped him get onto the straight and narrow, I knew I wanted to work with you."

"Your father spoke of us in a sermon?" I was almost afraid to ask. "What's his name?"

"The most Revered Minister Freddie Jackson." Marilyn replied.

I shook my head. "All right, all right." I said. "You convinced me. Steve, you do have another intern, don't neglect one over the other."

"I won't." Steve assured me.

"You tell Joe yet?" I asked.

"I was hoping you would tell him for me," Steve replied.

I took a breath. "So anyway," I changed the subject, "any news on the girl you were looking for?"

"Susan?" Steve said. "I found her."

"We found her," Marilyn interjected.

Steve rolled his eyes, and I was already feeling sorry for him.

"We found her," Steve finally agreed. "And passed the message to her that her mother wanted to talk to her."

"Did they talk?" I asked.

"Not at first," Steve replied. "I had to catch up to her a couple of more times before she agreed to meet her mom at Sloppy's over an early dinner."

"So they had a long talk," I commented. "Did it take?"

"Dunno." Steve said. "The mom dismissed me as soon as they met. Paid up for the services."

"I know what happened!" Marilyn excitedly interjected.

"I had Marilyn sitting in the booth behind me," Steve said, "She was there for everything after I left. She was just about to fill me in on what happened when you dropped by."

I looked to Marilyn and she smiled. "Well," Marilyn took a deep breath and then said, "Well, after you got kicked out," she glanced at

Steve then continued talking and making eye contact with me, making sure I knew who was making the report, "they began talking. And the mom was being all calm and cautious and saying sweet things to her daughter, then the girl just shut it down and asked, 'What do you want from me?' And the mom said she just wanted her to come home and such and that it would all be good, that she wanted them to be a family again and all and then the girl started asking what did Dave think about it, and the mom said, 'Dave has nothing to do with it,' and the girl said Dave had everything to do with it and that Dave had everything to do with everything since he came into their life and didn't the mom realize that he was the one who forced her to run away? Then the mom got all defensive and such and started to defend this Dave guy, saying, oh he's a sweet man, and he means the best and she just doesn't understand him, and then the girl said she does understand, and that she has eyes and that her mom has blinders on and she doesn't see what is happening in front her face and she has been telling her mom, over and over about how abusive this Dave character is to her and to her mom and her mom just won't listen. And then the girl starts getting on about how her real dad never treated either of them that way and that her mom was a terrible mom for letting this Dave guy come into their lives. And then the mom gets on ragging about the girl's father, how horrible he was and that she just doesn't remember and so on, and then the girl says that this Dave guy tried to touch her and then it just went quiet for a few moments. Then the mom started saying that the girl was lying and how horrible it was for her to make up such a story and if she was younger she would wash her mouth out with soap, and then the girl broke down crying, saying the mom just wasn't listening to her and that she never listened to her and how she hated her and she hated her life, and she just got up and ran out of Sloppy's."

"Wow!" Steve said and I just nodded. It was similar to stories I'd heard replayed a thousand times in the Tenderloin. Sad. Just plain sad.

"Good. Thanks for the recap," I said plainly. Marilyn was new and I didn't want her to get over confident. "Write up an abbreviated and clean version and add it to the case's computer file. Steve," I said, "Do a follow up call next week. Just to check in with our client, the girl's mom. Even if we've been paid, I like to know the final results before we close a case—if the girl went home, though I doubt that she will. If the mom says the girl is staying out here, reassure her that we'll keep an eye out for her. Which you will do, capische?"

Marilyn pulled out a small hand flip notebook, just like the type of notebook I carry, and wrote down a couple of words. "Got it," Marilyn said.

"Got it," confirmed Steve.

I straightened my suit jacket, went over to Steve and patted him on the arm as I whispered, "I think you now have your hands full with this one," in reference to Marilyn.

Steve just looked back at me, doe-eyed.

"And get this place organized." I ordered, "I don't want to see open cabinets or dust the next time I come in."

"Yup." Steve said.

"Nice to meet you, Marilyn," I said as I went over to shake her hand. "Welcome to the company."

"Thank you!" Marilyn said as she aggressively shook my hand. "And so nice to make your acquaintance, Mr. Mason. And you'll see—I'll get this placed whipped into shape in no time."

"I'm sure you will," I said. "And just call me Mike."

"Okay, Mike," Marilyn smiled. "I will."

"And one more thing." I said as I was heading out the door, "All this stuff about reopening an old case, the one on Thomas Ballard, Joe's dad. I wouldn't say anything to Joe about it. Okay? Not right now, at least. Just keep me informed and let me know if there are any developments. Though I believe your chances of finding anything new on such an old case are slim to none."

14

WHEN I LEFT THE Tenderloin office that evening, my head was absolutely spinning. What a crazy day—from the morning researching Amado's life, to the afternoon with Colin playing his games, to the evening where I found out Steve had hired a new intern, Marilyn. I needed a drink, bad, and wanted to be alone, so I caught a taxi home, ordered in, poured myself a couple of drinks and blankly watched some television to decompress.

That night, Rich called me, but I didn't pick it up or return her call. She called me again the next day and that evening as well, but I didn't return her messages. I was pissed at just about everything that centered around her. I was pissed that Colin apparently had a boss that was watching me, for some unknown reason, and wanted to make a point that he knew just about everything in my life. I was pissed that they were trying to use my past to control me. I was pissed that the fat bastard Colin had been playing me like a child, then seemed to want me as a nanny. But most of all, what I was pissed about, was Rich, Rich and her husband that I hadn't known about.

The whole incident had put me in such a foul mood I felt I had to make some changes and to take a break. The first change was to update my bedroom door handle from a lever style to the round door knob Joe had given me; Poseidon would no longer be able to jump and pull down on the handle to open it and I would get a full and good night's sleep. For the break, it was nearing the weekend and I decided I'd take a little trip down to Coastanoa, a camping spa just past the small coastal town of Pescadero. I awoke early that Friday morning to change my door handle and then headed out first toward our Pacifica office, hoping to catch Joe to give him a heads-up before heading out.

As I headed for my car, my mood already was moving toward the positive. I also felt that over the past few days, there seemed to be a change in the mood of Pacifica. It seemed that outside in the larger world, the scent of gold was dying down. The Coastal Watch hadn't printed anything over the past week on the hunt for gold and I took it that the gold fever had broke. For me, although I was no longer interested in the hunt for gold, I already decided I'd continue the quest for Amado. His life and times were intriguing. It would be one of my side projects, maybe to help me forget Rochelle, or Rich as I now preferred to call her.

I left my house, driving down Oddstad Boulevard, then onto Linda Mar and was passing Sanchez Adobe when I caught that the gate to the parking lot was open. It had to be Daniel in there. It was actually too early to be open, but I figured he probably had spent the night. I decided I'd drop in on him. He was a character and I liked him. He had a good spirit. I also thought I'd talk to him a little bit more about Amado. Maybe it would give me something to ponder as I hung out at my cabin in Pescadero. I made a U-turn a half block down and came back around to pull into the adobe parking lot. There I found Daniel's old black Schwinn ten-speed locked to the bike rack and as I approached the adobe, I could see the thick wooden door of the place was partially open.

Something wasn't right. It was too quiet, so at the entrance to the adobe, I stopped and as quietly and as slowly as possible and with the nail of one fingertip, I pushed the door open wide. The room was dark but as sunlight entered the room with the opening of the door, I could see a couple of things, legs sprawled out on the floor, and bloody partial right footprints leaving the adobe.

I stepped back for a moment. No matter how often I've come across someone who is dead, it always takes me a moment to catch my breath. I now noticed the partial bloody right footprints continued outside and headed around to the corner of the adobe and into the lawn where they disappeared in the fog moistened grass.

I went back and entered, making sure I didn't step on the footprints as I made my way to the body on the floor. It was Daniel. He was lying in a puddle of his blood on the floor. He was dead.

I pulled out my phone, searched through my contacts and pulled the number programmed in my phone for the Pacifica police. I told the operator that I found someone dead at the Sanchez Adobe and asked if she could send someone right away. I knew a couple of cars would be there within minutes. There is always a pair at the Starbucks in the Linda Mar Shopping Center at this time of the morning.

I knelt down next to Daniel and looked more closely at his face. That sweet countenance was replaced by the cold pallor of death.

The back of his head appeared to be the main source of blood that had drained onto the floor; however, his forehead also had received some trauma. Smack-dab in the middle of his forehead, a black, red and purple bruise was still forming, as blood trickled out in little rivulets. The bruise itself was circular and about half dollar in size and from previous experience, had the tell-tale signs of being the result of a hammer attack.

I stepped out of the room and adobe just as two police cars pulled up. They were soon followed by an ambulance, several more police cars, several plainclothes cops and in the immediate hours that followed, reporters, news vans and onlookers. The questions were the same, consistent, and asked over and over again, retracing my steps that morning until the time I came across the body. Had I met Daniel before and under what circumstances? Was I working a case for him?

It wasn't until Pacifica Police captain Tony Chin arrived and went round with me with similar questions that I was finally let in on some additional information—that although Daniel was generally well liked, he did have some problems that had previously brought him to the police's attention. It was a little matter of domestic violence, and his ex-wife was going to be picked up and interrogated. I was allowed to leave with the caveat that I stay as close as possible to Pacifica and within easy contact.

It was now close to eight in the evening and my whole day and plans for a restful weekend were shot. I also needed a drink and was hungry. I headed over to Cheers, had a couple of shots, then stepped outside and called Joe.

"Yeah," Joe answered. "Missed you this morning."

"I know," I said. "Couldn't help it. I had walked into a place with a body."

"Who?" Joe said plainly. "Where? Over in the Tenderloin?"

"Daniel Clay," I replied. "A docent over here at the Sanchez Adobe. Did you do a job for him awhile back?"

"Yeah," Joe said. "Just a quick, simple tail, photo and phone trace job. Wife was banging some guy. He was really broken up about it. Just came to the office, picked up the package, didn't even open it, started crying, paid and left. Poor guy. I heard all the sirens earlier this morning." Joe said, "I'm guessing you knew him?"

"Just met him the other day," I replied. "Gave me some info about Amado."

"Who?" Joe asked.

"Amado. You know, as in Armando's gold. The gold coin. He was also called Amado."

"Never heard him called that before," Joe said. "You think anything you're doing got Daniel killed?"

"Not sure," I said. "Police are leaning toward it might be in the realms of domestic."

"Yup."

"Hey, where you at?" I asked. "Want to get a bite?"

"Can't right now," Joe said. "I'm futzing around down in the Stanford library. Seeing what I can find out about the gold rush and our friend Armando—I mean Amado. Oh, but I did hear back from the County Museum in Redwood City. The coin that I found was indeed gold and nothing they had really ever seen before. Said it looked homemade and had the all the hallmarks, by the design, that it was a primitive homemade job and put it around 1860. After they cleaned it, they said they wouldn't even call it a coin. More like just a small gold disc. I just picked it up today and decided to head down to Stanford since I was in the area to see if they could tell me anything. And oh, it did have some markings on it."

"What sort of markings?" I asked.

"A cross was on each side," Joe said. "Wasn't an accident. It was part of the mold that made it."

"Interesting," I said, then continued, "Oh yeah, so the other day I went over to the Fairmont and the Tonga Room to meet up with Rich's partner, remember?"

"Rich the fortune hunter gal?" Joe asked. "The one I warned you about?"

"Yeah," I said, deciding to come clean with my recent activities. "So Rich and I had been going about, looking more into the history of Amado and the history of the gold. We had checked out the Adobe together, met up with Daniel, which led us to Moses . . ."

"Moses Brown?" Joe interrupted.

"You know him?" I asked.

"Yeah," Joe said. "He's a Moose Lodge member."

"Nice guy," I said. "He told us a lot about Amado. His grandfather personally knew him."

"Really!" Joe was excited. "Well I'll be . . . yeah, well, it makes sense. His family has been here for quite a long time. And he was just telling me the other day how he remembers back near where you live, in Sun Valley, when it was still countryside, then later after Terra Nova High School was built, there was this big culvert he'd walk his dog through to go down to Saint Peter's. I'll have to ask him about Amado."

"Anyway," I continued, "we also stopped in at Mission Dolores, remember? And I found out a bit more about Amado." I now filled in Joe about the Mission binders, what we found out about Amado, about his life at the Mission through his running off to the gold fields. I then went on about my meeting with Colin and Rich and about the letter that contained details of my life. Somehow, or for some reason, I ended it there, deliberately leaving out telling Joe about the feelings I had for Rich, and the part about her husband, and afterwards. Maybe there were still some latent feelings in me about her or maybe I didn't want to look like a sap in front of my friend. In any event, I ended with, "So what do you make of that?' in reference to the letter that contained my life's story.

"Interesting," Joe said. "Sounds like this Colin fellow, or his boss, is trying to strong arm you."

"Yeah, but for what purpose?" I asked. "It just ended there. Didn't seem much of a reason for it, except to say, 'I have my eye on you.'"

"Do you think Rich is in on it?" Joe asked.

"I'm not convinced," I said. "Seems like she is more of the lackey in the relationship. And oh, get this, I saw Steve the other day, as well. He hired another intern."

There was silence on the other end for a few moments. "Paid?" Joe asked.

"No. Not yet. But there seems like there are some expectations. She's good. Motivated. And Steve did need the help. I think he was beginning to get overwhelmed trying to keep the paper part of the business going while trying to establish himself."

"I guess I approve," Joe said, "as she's already working there."

"And oh, one more thing," I said. "She's the daughter of Freddie Jackson."

"Gawd!" Joe said, then after a few moments, "I guess I still approve. It might help cement our place within the community. And he supposedly turned over a new leaf. We just need to watch and see if the apple fell far enough away from the tree."

When I hung up with Joe, I took a couple of paces back and forth before I decided it was time that I called Rich.

"Long time, no hear," Rich said.

"Where you at?" I asked.

"REI Sporting Goods," she said. I could hear music in the background and guessed she was telling the truth.

"Daniel is dead," I blurted out to try to catch any reaction from her.

"What?" She did sound as if she was in shock. "What happened?"

"He got hammered," I said.

"Drank himself to death?" she asked. "Crashed his car?"

"No," I said plainly, "someone went at him with a hammer."

"Jesus," Rich said.

I was silent, waited to see if she would talk more. She did. "Well I guess there are people out there, a lot of people out there, who might be interested in the information he might have."

"That's sort of a funny comment," I said. "Thinking it is related to the gold?"

"Well, isn't that what you think?" she asked.

"Police think it might have been his ex," I said.

"Oh," Rich said. "I guess they have their reasons."

"Yeah," I replied and waited. I pictured in my mind that as we talked, she stopped what she was doing, maybe was standing in the coat aisle, one hand with the phone to the ear, the other motionless as it touched a coat on the rack.

She wasn't saying anything so I continued, "So is there anything you want to talk to me about?"

"No. Not that I can think of," Rich replied.

"Well it looks like you called me a couple of times, a few days ago," I said.

"Did I? I can't remember," she said.

"Nothing about the other day—about our meeting with your friend Colin?"

"Oh, well, I was interested why you ran out the other day." She said, "Throwing the table and running out of there like a bat out of hell."

"I'm sure you know why." I said.

"No, I don't. I really don't." She pleaded innocence, "Colin didn't tell me a thing."

"Nothing? Really," I said, "He never told you that he spilled the beans that you had a husband? That you were married?"

"A husband?" Rich sounded surprised.

"Yes. The one you never mentioned," I stated flatly.

"I don't know what you're talking about." Rich whined.

"Really!" I said.

"Really!" Rich said. "Look, I don't know what Colin told you, but I am definitely not married. And I really don't know what you two talked about. He didn't tell me a thing. After you stormed out, he was laughing hysterically and just said that apparently you couldn't take a joke. I asked him what he said to you, and he just brushed me off. That's his way. He always does things like that. He likes playing jokes on people. It's one of the little games he plays."

"Well you can tell him I'm definitely not into those sort of games." I replied.

"I think he understands that from your reactions." Rich said, "Listen Mike, I know Colin can be crass and crude sometimes, but he really isn't that bad of a fellow."

"You know, Rich," I said, "there's a saying about the people one tends to associate with, birds of a feather."

"Are you calling me crass and crude?" Rich asked.

"No," I said, "I'm just not sure how to take you. If you like playing games. If I'm someone you are toying with."

"No Mike," Rich's voice softened. "It's not that way at all. I do like you. I think we make a good team. I brought you to Colin because I had spoken to him about you, and I like working with you and I thought that maybe he would be interested in employing you in the future. We could work together as a team."

"So it wasn't Colin's idea, to see about bringing me on board?" I asked.

"No, I suggested that he meet you. I told him a little bit about you, how you were good about piecing things together and how well we worked well together."

"And what about Colin's employer?" I asked, "He had nothing to do with me meeting with Colin?"

"I didn't know he even knew you existed."

"Really." I said unsure whether to believe her, "Well, is there anything you can tell me about him? Who is he? What's his name?"

"I don't know his name," Rich said, "I only met him once, when I first started working with Colin. Colin said he had a financier and he wanted to meet me."

"Well, describe him?" I said, "What did he look like?"

"Well, I never actually saw him," Rich continued. "Colin brought me to his place, an office downtown and just left me in a room that had a big two-way mirror, a microphone and speaker. Then a voice came over the speaker and I started getting asked questions."

"By who? Colin?"

"No, his financier." Rich replied. "I was alone in the room and he was on the other side, and he asked me a whole series of questions."

"What kind of questions?"

"I don't know. They seemed silly." Rich said, "Sort of like those questions you see on psychological tests you took in college, to check your personality, like what's your favorite color."

"That's it?" I asked.

"Well, yeah," Rich said. "After the last question, I waited for a few minutes then Colin came in and said all was good and we left."

"Anything else you can remember?" I asked. "What did his voice sound like? What impression did it give you? Did he have an accent?"

Rich paused for a moment. I could just about hear the clicking of the gears in her head as she tried to access the memory. For the moment, it seemed she was trying to be honest.

"I don't remember an accent," she finally said. "And his voice was very static, straight forward, literally no inflection. He could have been short, tall, thin or large. It was just a very clear voice."

"Do you remember where this all took place? Downtown? You said downtown. What part of downtown, the theater district, the financial district?"

"It was down on Market Street." Rich said, "Kinda close to the Ferry Building. On the right-hand side if you are facing the Ferry Building on Market Street."

"Was it a tall or short building?" I asked.

"Tall. It was one of those really tall ones." Rich said, "And his office is way up near the top."

"Is it an older or newer building?"

"Newer."

"All glass or a lot of cement? Did it have a plaza? What was the general outside color of the building?"

"I can't remember." She sounded frustrated.

"If I took you down there, downtown, do you think you could point out the building?"

"Maybe," Rich said, "Mike, what's this about?"

"Colin's employer had looked into my past, into the details of my life. He put it down on paper and it seems he is trying to intimidate me. I don't like that." Just recounting that to Rich was getting my ire up.

"I don't believe he was trying to intimidate you." Rich defended her bosses. "I think they were just checking you out. Doing a background check, in a way, to see if you'd fit in with us."

"Well I," I said, "I don't like the way I would fit into your little group. The way I see it, Colin has an employer and he is Colin's puppet master. You work for Colin, so Colin is your puppet master. What would that make me if I worked for your group, or for you?"

"Mike, you wouldn't work for me. We could work as partners."

"Not in this scheme of things." I said, "Look, I would be the lowest man on this totem pole, I don't like the way this stacks up."

"Mike, I'm really sorry about anything Colin may have said to upset you, but he really meant no harm. That's just his way. You can't imagine how many times he's played jokes on me or said things that were totally inappropriate. Sometimes the things he does infuriate me, but he is also my boss. He pays my bills so I let things pass and I also go back to that's just his way. Once you understand that, you'll see he's really an okay guy."

"Well, there's a difference,' I said, "You go along and play his games, for he's your boss. He's not mine. I don't have to put up with his shit."

There was a long pause on the other end of the phone. I'm sure I had been raising my voice, sounding more and more frustrated and when I swore, I think that was the conversation killer.

"Look Mike, I have to go," Rich finally said.

"Wait a minute. Hold on," I said. "So what is it?"

"What?" Rich said.

"Your favorite color?" I asked in reference to the question that was asked of Rich by Colin's employer.

Rich took a breath and paused. "It used to be red, but right now, I think blue is my color. That is how I feel right now. What's yours?"

"Orange," I simply replied.

When I hung up the phone with Rich, my head was spinning again. She had given me some information, but still not enough to have anything to go on in regards to Colin's employer and as to why he was looking into my past. I checked my watch and it was getting pretty late and I was absolutely famished, so I decided to try the fare over at Vallamar Station, the old train depot where Rich and I had met up with Moses. I made it just in time for the last dinner service before they shut the restaurant portion and left the bar side open until the end of the night. I had a porterhouse and rice and by the time I was done, the karaoke in the bar had started. I paid my tab and joined the crowd in the bar. I ordered a Manhattan and listened as a trio of young girls sang Abba's "Money, Money, Money." Yeah, I thought to myself, that is what the whole world is about.

As the night went on, I began to get a feeling that something wasn't right and was feeling some personal responsibility for Daniel's death. Maybe it was something that Rich had said. The line . . . *people might be interested in the information he might have.*

I checked the phone records on my phone and found the number for Moses Brown from the time when Daniel had called him. I selected the number and called Moses. There was no answer.

I hung up the phone before the answering machine came on. It was late and Moses was old. He probably was sleeping. I called him again anyway—still no answer. I decided to give it a rest for the night and decided just to enjoy myself, shake off the day by singing a couple of songs.

When I finally left Vallamar Station at two in the morning, I headed straight down Highway One. I took the longer route, bypassing Fassler and instead opting to drive up Linda Mar Boulevard to take a long last look at Sanchez Adobe before going to bed. When I arrived, I saw the yellow police tape was still up and the single light Daniel used to leave on was off. I parked down the street and walked back to the adobe. The last few days had been gloomy, very gray and cold outside, matching the way I had been feeling, but tonight you could see the sky was clearing.

I crossed the police line, went around the gate, and headed down the path to reach the adobe, where I found more police tape; however, it appeared to have been pulled off the doorframe, as if someone had dropped by after the police had left. I stopped and listened, putting my ear to the door. Silence. I slowly cracked the door open with my fingernails and listened. Still nothing. I then opened the door wide enough to enter and close it behind me. I fished out the mini-magnum light that is attached to my key chain and began to look around.

First I looked at the floor where I had seen Daniel lay earlier in the day. There was a chalk outline and the blood was still pooled on the floor. The place, the drying blood, made the room smell like death. I began to shine my flashlight around the edges of the floor toward the walls, and that is when I first started to notice it: specks of white on the floor. I shined my light onto the walls and found spots where the cement had been hit with what apparently was a hammer, knocking off some paint. I went closer to the far wall: a few of the strikes appeared to have been made with the same hammer that had been used on Daniel, blows of round circular spheres fading into thinning red blood crescents. I checked my memory. I didn't remember seeing the walls having been struck when I first came upon Daniel's body.

I checked the other rooms on the ground floor and in both, especially in the corners, it looked as if hammer blows had struck against the wall with little effect. These interior walls on the first floor were not just a thin coating of cement but thick solid shotcrete walls, made during the reconstruction and preservation that was first attempted by the county sometime after it purchased the property back in 1947. These lower floor interior walls were basically impenetrable and I'm guessing at some point, the culprit or culprits probably realized it.

I went outside and headed upstairs. The door on the second floor had a broken glass pane and the door itself was unlocked and slightly open. I pushed the door open wide with my fingernails and entered, again using my flashlight to scan the area. In these upstairs rooms, the floors were littered with bits of plaster and whitewash paint from obvious hammer blows to the walls. The blows appeared random in placement, as if someone was testing the strength of the walls. I stepped back outside and looked down the length of the veranda and could see that there was some damage to the outside of the adobe. I walked the veranda and when I reached the end of the building, I found that almost each and every adobe brick had been slammed hard with a hammer, cracking many of them. The concentration of the damage appeared to be in the corners of the building, with some of the bricks having been completely demolished. Then it struck me as hard as a hammer blow.

I ran downstairs to check the outside of the adobe at both ends of the building, when I came across what I was half expecting to see: an area where the bricks had been broken and removed, revealing a small cavity lined on all sides within the adobe itself. "Son of a bitch," I said aloud.

I headed out and climbed into my car, where I called Joe. It took several redials to get him to pick up.

"What's going on?" Joe sounded annoyed, as I surely had just awoken him from sleep.

"I just came from the adobe," I said, "and whoever killed Daniel returned."

Joe just grunted.

"Something else," I continued. "Whoever it was, found something."

"The map!" Joe said suddenly, as if being struck by lightning.

"Probably," I said. "I don't know for sure. But there were some bricks that were removed and it looks like there is a hollow space behind them."

Joe was silent and I could just about hear the wheels in his head turning. "You think you know who did it?" he asked.

"Rich and her partner," I replied.

Joe agreed.

"When I talked to Rich the other day, she mentioned she was at REI Sporting Goods."

"Getting outfitted with additional supplies," Joe concluded.

"No doubt," I agreed.

There was a long pause then Joe yawned and said, "Well, there's really nothing we can do until morning." He yawned again. "Get some sleep. I'll call you as soon as I get up."

"All right," I said, knowing full well that Joe was going to be up the rest of the night, thinking and preparing himself for the following day.

I headed home, where I was greeted by Poseidon who made walking figure eights between my legs, meowing and looking up at me as I tried to move. He'd been especially affectionate, plying me to pet him since he'd been permanently locked out of my bedroom. I finally picked him up, draped him over my shoulder as I turned on my living room television for background noise, and trudged upstairs.

I went into my second bedroom that I've converted into an office. It has a couple of walnut bookcases and a combination HP printer-scanner-copier-fax machine that barely fit on a small folding table. My laptop was on a cherry colored tiny work desk I had picked up years ago from Staples. This room was also Poseidon's *designated* bedroom. He had a cat scratching post he didn't use, a round beige colored rug covered sleeping box he didn't use, and a folding futon he did use. The futon pad closest to my computer was my extended desk. Emails, notes and invoices from Steve and now Marilyn, filled a good portion of it.

Most of the time when I was in my office, Poseidon would lay on the top of the futon and looked out the window that backed the futon but tonight, since I was now working at my desk, he was busy rubbing his cheeks on the edge of my monitor, his orange fur slowly being sucked into my laptop, slowly clogging its cooling fan, one orange strand at a time.

I downloaded the San Francisco North USGS topographic quadrangle at 1:24,000 that contains San Pedro County Park. I'd always been a map buff and I found looking at the map exciting. So many places to explore. Opportunities to discover something new . . . once this current matter had been resolved.

The printer started chugging, shaking the little folding table it was perched upon until the print was complete. I looked at the map. Montara Mountain was ruggedly dramatic, rising nearly two thousand feet from sea level, and made up of fiercely weathered granites and sedimentary assemblages. It was also faulted throughout, being so close to the San Andreas, making for some spectacular fault gorges into the mountain.

I placed the map onto the futon and began to search the 'Net for more info about the mountain, to see if I could determine the most likely location of a cave. Poseidon jumped off my desk and I heard him nestle onto the futon. I checked satellite images of San Pedro County Park and the bordering areas. I checked websites about the park, and park brochures that detailed the trails in the park and the park itself.

There was nothing that stood out to say, "This is where a cave can be found," so I decided to use reverse logic, rule out areas where I didn't think a cave could exist; areas I remembered from walking where the hillsides were just that, hillsides. I marked off areas where there was little vegetation or where I could see there was too much foot traffic from hikers. When I was done, I was still left with the majority of the mountain and numerous valleys that needed to be explored.

I looked over my shoulder to check in on Poseidon. He was laying on the futon, all right, but he had his paws on the map I had placed there, enjoying the warmth of a freshly printed page. When he saw me looking at him, he began to knead the sheet, so I snatched it out of his paws. "Poseidon!" I yelled. I then inspected the sheet to see what damage he had caused and found only one place where one of Poseidon's' nails had pierced the map. I patched the map by pushing the paper back flat from behind and then inspected the damaged area again.

The hole that Poseidon had made was in one of the most dramatic fault gorges in the park, a valley that contained sheer walls on one side and rounded hills on the other. I checked the topographic map against one of the park's brochures. The park brochure showed there was a single track trail on the more rounded hillside that skirted the valley. The trail was called the Brooks Falls trail and was developed in the mid 1980s, but the general area—it made sense to me. In Amado's time, the area was accessible in distance from the adobe, but there were areas that were clearly inaccessible due to the general topography and the thick vegetation of the area.

I looked to Poseidon. "So you think the area near Brooks Falls is the place to look?" He just looked into my eyes and I went over and rubbed his head.

"Good kitty." I said, then pulled a cover out from the closet and laid it on the futon for Poseidon to sleep. I then went to my bedroom, closing the door to keep Poseidon out. My bedroom window looked out toward the rugged Manzanita and Madrone covered Montara Mountain. The profile of the mountain was that of a jagged saw blade in the moon-filled sky. Though I've hiked many trails within the park, I've always wanted to hike to the top of the mountain. I just never found the time. Maybe the next day was to be that time.

WEEK IV

15

IN THE MORNING, I awoke to Posideon banging at the door, trying to get in. I think he was throwing his body against it, or jumping up at the door knob. I dressed in my long army green Carhartt cargo pants, Alpine hiking boots, Patagonia shirt and Northface jacket, grabbed the topographic map of San Pedro County Park I had printed the night before, folded it and placed it in my back pocket. Poseidon needed some morning hug time, then his food. Once he was fed, I was allowed to leave with him licking his chops, watching me leave through the back glass slider.

I hopped into my car and met Joe in the San Pedro County Park parking lot. When I arrived, I also spotted Rich's van. Joe came up to my car and was waiting for me as I opened my door.

"Moses is dead," Joe said.

"Dead?" I was in shock.

"The official word isn't out yet," Joe said, "but it looks like he was crushed and his head nearly chopped off."

"Jeez, crushed and beheaded." I said. "Any murder weapons?"

"Haven't found any yet," Joe said.

"Who found him?" I asked.

"Moses was a very active member of the Moose Lodge. One of his friends dropped by Moses' place when he missed a couple of functions, and found him in his living room. Said at first he actually looked peaceful, laid back in a recliner with a cover up to his chin. The guy thought he was just sleeping at first when he saw him, but when he removed the cover to check his chest for a heartbeat, he found that his chest covered in blood and caved in."

"Gawd," I said. "I see Rich's van is here."

"Yeah," Joe said. "I checked it out. Hood is still a little warm, so she can't be too far ahead of us. You packing?"

"No," I said.

"I didn't think of it, either." Joe said. "Think I should make an office run and bring out the Barbies?" Barbies are what we refer to when we are talking about our Berettas. I can't recall who came up with the name or how it came about. We've just been calling them that for years.

"Naw," I said. "I think we're okay. If they are responsible for both Daniel and Moses' deaths, they didn't use guns."

"Agreed," Joe said. "If they had guns, they probably would have used them. But there's still a chance. And they at least used a hammer on Daniel and some sort of knife on Moses. I'm going to make a quick run back to the office."

"All right," I said. "I'm going to be starting up the Brooks Falls trail." I pulled out the map from my back pocket. "The trailhead is supposed to be over here somewhere. Maybe I can catch a glimpse of Rich before she gets too far ahead."

"You can start over there." Joe pointed over to a set of restrooms. "There's a trail on the side of that. Just follow it and watch the signs. There's a bench that overlooks the falls; wait for me there or when the trail hooks up with the fire trail. You can't miss that one. Nice bench where the two trails meet, one that overlooks Pacifica."

Joe hopped into his truck and headed to our office, and I began the hike. Fog capped the mountain top and I could see it was making its way down toward the valleys, but I supposed I wouldn't get too cold, not with hiking. The trail was pleasant enough at first, not too steep and surrounded by wildflowers, but soon it began to climb, fast and steep. I put my hands on my hips as I walked, out of shape for this kind of workout. I wasn't paying attention to what was too far in front of me, paying more attention to the cliffside on my left and making sure my footsteps on the trail were sure. Eucalyptus leaves littered a portion of the trail, followed by pine cones, then as the trail made a turn along a cliffside overlooking a valley, the foliage turned to grass and finally an overgrowth of Manzanita and Madrone with their nice red peeling bark. A few more turns and the valley below me began to get squeezed into a steep and impenetrable "v" shape, the opposing cliffs rising high above the side I was hiking upon with warm thermal updrafts that made a playground for circling California vultures.

The trail twisted and turned onward and with the Manzanita and Madrone, and I soon found myself hunched over trying to avoid the low branches. Then on a sharp turn, the vegetation cleared and I found myself at the base of an upturned bowl-shaped gravelly rise bare of vegetation and upon it, was a fat man on a bench staring across the valley at the opposing cliff face. The man was wearing white Nike shoes with long white socks that covered his calves, tight white shorts and a beige short sleeve shirt that was dripping with sweat. A walking stick was by his side, leaning against the bench. He was sweating like a fat pig roasting on a spit above a fire. He was sitting there gasping, sweat pouring off his head. I recognized him immediately. It was Colin Broadmore.

Colin was looking through a set of binoculars with its plastic strap looped around his neck. I tried to look to the area he was looking at, and it seemed he was looking out towards a waterfall far off and across to the other side of the valley. The water falling from the falls was minimal, and it appeared to fall in several stages, often disappearing in the foliage and cliff face. I squinted and tried to see even further as to what Colin might be looking at but the sun and glare were bright and when I refocused my gaze back to Colin, he was glaring right at me.

"Well hello, Colin," I called out. "Fancy meeting you here!" I started to move towards him.

"I mark that this isn't a coincidental meeting," Colin said, "and indeed, I believe your arrival to be a most inopportune distraction."

"Where's your little weasel?" I asked.

"If you mean where's my lovely associate," Colin replied laughing, "you need to look no farther than across the valley, somewhere over by the waterfall, although I haven't been able to spot her for quite some time."

"Fine enough," I said. "If she finds anything, I'll get it out of her when she climbs off this mountain and prior to sending her to prison as a murderer or as an accomplice to the murders of both Daniel and Moses. For you, right now, the game is over."

Colin rose off the bench and pulled the rubber stopper off the end of his walking stick to reveal a silver spike. He now held his walking stick as a spear and pointed it toward me. I continued towards him and him towards me until we were just out of each other's reach. Colin was gritting his teeth, readying himself for a fight and I watch as large drops of sweat made their way from underneath his hat and down his forehead. When they reached his eyes, causing him to blink, I would rush him, swatting at and then grabbing the end of his walking stick.

A moment passed, and when Colin blinked, I rushed him. We began tussling over the walking stick, sliding on the uneven ground. Back and forth side to side we fought for control of the stick, then I started pushing Colin back hard, using all of my strength, directing this enormous human mound of blubber back towards the bench. He in turn, increased his attack, nearly ripping my arm out of its socket as he yanked the walking stick from side to side as we wrestled for control. Then, right before one of his massive yanks of the pole, I gambled and released my hold. That was all it took.

Letting go allowed Colin's weight to wield him around and being on uneven and a gravelly surface, he slipped and fell, landing head first, pointing down the slope, toward the cliff edge and the valley far below. I rested for a moment and Colin tried to roll on his side to get up, but he began sliding toward the cliff edge. Each time he tried to move, to roll to get up, the conveyor belt of little round gravel rocks would move him a little faster down the increasingly steeper slope and towards the edge of the cliff.

"Try not to move!" I shouted to Colin, and for a moment, he listened as he tried to catch his breath, his hands trying to dig into the hillside, but only scratching the rock surface and getting hold of little weathered granite pebbles.

I carefully moved toward Colin, staying low as the angle of the slope would have pitch me forward and over the cliff if I stood straight. I also thought about grabbing Colin by the hand but thought better as he might just grab me and yank me over the cliff. So instead, I grabbed at what was initially closest to me, the binoculars' plastic strap that was around his neck. I thought at least with a hand on this, I could slow his slide towards the cliff however when I grabbed at it, the strap immediately began to strangle him and he reached at his neck. The strain broke the strap and Colin began sliding faster towards the edge of the cliff.

"Help me! Help me!" Colin began screaming.

I now grabbed at Colin's right leg but could only get a portion of my hands around his huge right ankle. He was gaining momentum on his slide and now gravity was really beginning to take control, pulling me down as well, both of us sliding towards the cliff. I fell to my butt, trying to dig my feet in but was unable to do so in the gravel covered rock surface. I leaned back, straining to hold onto Colin, trying to keep the both of us from sliding over the cliff when I heard Joe yell "Mike!"

"Joe," I yelled desperately and found him to be behind me, one hand grabbing the bench, the other outstretched toward me. My choice was now to release one hand from being wrapped around Colin's ankle and reach out to Joe, or hold onto Colin and get pulled down and off the cliff face with him. I released one hand and stretched toward Joe.

At first our fingertips just touched but eventually we got a fireman's lock on each other's wrist. Meanwhile, my grip on Colin was slipping. I released my grip that was now slicked with sweat from his leg and got a handhold of shoe. Colin began to panic.

"Help me! Help me!" He cried out as he began to roll.

My fingers began to bet twisted in my hold of him as he rolled and I could feel his shoe begin to be pulled off his foot. I had to adjust my hold. I released and now grabbed a hold of the tongue of his shoe as his ankle twisted. He responded by the pain of his twisting ankle by kicking.

"Stop that!" I yelled, "Stop kicking!" but Colin didn't and he managed to kick his shoe off and into my hand.

There was no stopping gravity now. Colin began slipping and actually turning to be more parallel to the cliff face. He hit a Manzanita sapling and for a split second I thought that would stay his fall, but then, either unknowingly or deliberately or by gravity, he just rolled over it, picked up speed and rolled off the cliff screaming all the way.

Colin's yells preceded grunts, groans and the breaking of Manzanita and Madrone branches as he fell to the valley far below. And then there was silence. Joe helped me to my feet and we both sat on the bench, catching our breath as the California vultures that were riding the thermals seemed to find something new of interest below them.

"Don't think he could have survived that, do you?" I said plainly as I dusted off myself and tried to get the blood circulating back into my hands.

"Doubt it," Joe casually said. He reached into his pocket and pulled out a chewed Magnolia cigar and put it in his mouth. He then reached into his waistband and pulled out a Beretta and handed it to me. "There's someone else on this mountain."

"I know," I said. "I'd like to do this alone."

"Good," Joe said. "'Cause I don't want to go hiking over kingdom come with you. Where are you planning to go?"

I pointed to where I saw Colin had been looking with his binoculars. "Over there."

The area looked extremely rugged and was nearly directly across the valley.

"Okay," Joe said. "I'm going to head back and will call 911. Let them know about Colin. Will probably be back at this spot with search and rescue in, I'd guess, two, maybe three hours. I'll tell them basically that I saw someone go off the cliff, which I did."

"Guess I don't have much time," I said.

"Be careful," Joe said.

"Will do."

16

From the bench on the Brooks Falls Trail, the path continued its climb up Montara Mountain. I now started running up the switchbacks, ducking under the branches of overgrown Manzanita and Madrone, rattlesnake grass whipping at my legs as I ran. I pride myself on being fairly in shape, but the heat and the incline was getting to me. When I reached the fire trail that led to the top of Montara Mountain, I paused at the bench that overlooked Pacifica and the Pacific Ocean to catch my breath and to rest my pounding heart. Beautiful. Blue sky and a blue ocean meeting a crescent shaped strip of white waves, beige sand and a small coastal town. I pulled out my topographic map and studied the contours, looking for the best route off the fire trail that would lead me around the head of the valley and to the other side, where I saw the waterfalls.

From the bench onward, the fire trail became a single track gully-filled trail, and my speed slowed as I had to watch my step to avoid twisting an ankle. A turn, a bend and another bend and I saw a break in the wall of Manzanita off to my side and took it to find a gravelly patch of rock. I could tell I was getting closer to the head of the valley, closer to the waterfall. I jumped back onto the trail and continued to follow it until it made a large bend and began the steepest series of switchbacks I had encountered thus far. I checked my map. I was now at the head of the valley, and it was time to follow tick covered deer trails which were everywhere, parting, merging and then parting again.

There was no telling which deer trail to take as sometimes they just doubled back on themselves and other times just disappeared. The terrain had also become quite rough and at some point I decided I had to make my own way, off-road it, with no marked trail, not even deer trails.

My pace was now a walk as I climbed over rocks and boulders, sometimes slinging and pushing branches away, stepping over stunted trees. I was not used to this type of climbing. I was overheating and thirsty, dripping sweat even with the coolness of the encroaching fog bringing down the overall ambient temperature.

As I hiked and climbed, I kept my eyes open for signs that someone had trampled through the area before me. There were no footprints, the ground being too rocky and filled with pebbles but I was beginning to see branches, bent or broken. My hunch had been correct; Rich had been this way, evident by more and more broken branches.

The terrain was also getting steeper and more slippery as I started to come across little rivulets of water. A little trickle here, a little trickle there, not enough to be part of the waterfall, but enough to wet the soles of my boots and to make my hike that much more dangerous.

As I hiked, I wondered how Joe was doing with the rescue personnel and thought that maybe they would be in time to rescue me. The path I was taking was becoming more and more vertical and more and more dangerous. The rock under my feet was becoming extremely slick, mossy, black and wet and I was finally in an area near what would be the waterfall. I could hear it, somewhere among the branches and below me.

Fog was now dripping down the slopes of the mountain and into the valley below me like milk being poured into a bowl and it was at this point that I saw it: a rock in the shape of a saddle horn with a green climbing rope wrapped around it. The other end of the rope dropped off a cliff face and blended into the Manzanita forest that clung to the side of the mountain. Carefully I made my way to the rock shaped like a saddle horn and the rope's anchor. I gently touched the rope; it looked and felt new and it wasn't taut so I knew that although no one was currently on it. I knew, however, somewhere near the end of that rope, would be Rich.

I took off my jacket and hung it on some crimson Manzanita branches; flaky red bark falling from the branches from where I hung it and the fog cooled air ran a quick chill across my sweaty body that I had to shake off.

I grabbed hold of the rope and started rappelling down the cliff face, weaving between this bush and that, trying to be quiet but knowing I was as quiet as bull in a china shop. Rich was bound to have heard me. Maybe she even had seen me. At some point, I wrapped one arm around the rope, had one foot on the base of a bush, and checked my gun. My arms were becoming weak and I wondered if Joe could see me but then realized I was now in too thick of a mountainside grove of Manzanita to be seen. I was in it too deep.

After climbing some forty feet, I found a small ledge, and I could see that it widened as I looked down the length of it. There were also branches, whole limbs that had recently been cut and cleared away to allow an easier passage along the ledge, and in the distance, I could see what looked like a portal, possibly a cave. I tried looking straight below me but couldn't see the valley floor, but looking out from the cliff to a part of the valley that I could see, I gauged I was probably around seven hundred feet from the valley floor. And at that moment I thought about Amado. How the heck could he have gotten up here? The steep trails, the thick vegetation—I could see how he would definitely have had a hard time getting here in his later years.

I stepped onto the ledge, let go of the rope, grabbed hold of some Manzanita branches, then carefully made my way along the ledge until I was able to almost walk normally as I made my way toward what I thought might be a cave.

As I got closer, I could see that it was indeed a cave, a small ledge cave, similar to caves found in the Southwest. It had obviously been created eons ago when a large slab of the weathered grandidierite had broken away from the cliff face. It was now completely concealed from the opposing side of the valley by the overgrowth of Manzanita and Madrone. I tried to look out towards the far side of the valley and in a small break of the foliage, I could see people milling about around a bench. It had to be Joe and rescuers making an attempt to reach Colin. I could see them, but with the overgrowth, I was sure they would not be able to see me. I continued down the cliff ledge I had been on, making my way to the cave entrance, to this alcove, where I found Rich expecting me.

"Colin is hurting something awful right now," I said as I entered the cave.

"Colin ain't hurting for nothing," Rich said, "I saw him as he fell toward the valley floor. He was a pin cushion of Manzanita and Madrone when he landed."

Rich was standing with the machete that she had used to hack her way to the cave, hanging off a hook on her belt. I looked around the cave. There were some baskets, one knocked over, and near the cave's edge, a wood, metal and stone contraption, some boulders that looked as if they had been stained with smoke from what I gathered was a small fire pit, and leaning against the back wall of the cave, was a small man, or the remains of a man dressed in dust and dirt covered pants, poncho and a sombrero of sorts.

"I see you found Amado," I said as I turned my eyes back to Rich. I could see a wild lust in her eyes and sweat was beading off her forehead, more than one could expect from the arduous climb to this cave and having been there for quite sometime. She had gold fever.

"He must have made it here and couldn't get out," Rich said.

"Or decided just to stay," I countered, as from where he was sitting he would have been able to look out upon the valley.

"Nice view," she said. "How'd you find this place?"

"My cat found it," I said, referring to Poseidon having placed a claw on my topographic map. When Rich gave me a quizzical look, I continued, "Dead reckoning. The other valleys are rounder, smoother, don't have the cliff faces that this one has. It's also more vegetated so it would be easier for a cave to remain concealed over the years. Then finally, this side of the valley, is ultimately the least accessible area on this mountain. And after that, it was a matter of hiking and eventually following a trail of broken branches. Your messy path led me here."

Rich nodded.

"That and the short trail of dead bodies you began to make," I continued. "So tell me, Rich, why did you kill Moses?"

"I didn't kill Moses," Rich said defensively, "Colin did."

"You were with him. You were at least an accessory to the crime."

"Look," Rich said, "I liked the old man. I tried to persuade him to tell us what he knew, where the map was hidden, but he refused. He knew where the map was and he wasn't going to tell anyone. You've met Colin. He is not the sort that takes 'no' too well for an answer. Well, we kept asking and he kept avoiding and even tried to get away. Eventually, Moses pushed the wrong buttons and Colin pushed him down into his chair, sat down on him and started to lean back into the chair. Moses struggled for a bit and Colin pushed back more. Finally Moses was giving in, saying a map was in the walls of the adobe and just after he said that, there was this quick popping sound and I saw Colin fall deeper into the chair. The chair was a recliner and we had a heck of a time to get that chair back into a sitting position with both of them on it and by the time we did, that was it. Colin got off Moses, and Moses was dying."

"So Colin crushed him and smothered him at the same time," I said.

"It was an accident," Rich said. "He didn't mean it to happen that way and we both just felt awful about it."

"So awful you finished the job by slicing his neck and leaving him there." I added.

"Not like that! He was suffering. It was horrible. I . . . Colin just put him out of his misery by slitting his throat. And I didn't want to leave him like that," Rich said solemnly. "So I put a cover on him and put his chair back."

"So considerate." I said glancing to the machete dangling from Rich's belt and wondering if that was the weapon used to finish off Moses, "And Daniel?"

"Now Daniel was something altogether different," Rich said, her demeanor changed to that of anger. "Colin and I had just started looking for the map, knocking on some bricks in the wall with our hammers, when he came up from behind and grabbed Colin in a choke hold. I tried to pull his arm off as they swung around the room, but he wouldn't let go. Think what you will of Colin, but I would not let someone choke him to death, so when I had the chance, I hit Daniel in the forehead with my hammer. I didn't mean to hit him so hard to kill him, I just wanted him to let go. And he did let go, grabbing at his forehead and then, well, Colin picked up his hammer that he dropped in the struggle and he hit Daniel squarely in the back of the head. Daniel dropped and blood gushed out from behind him and we left."

"Only to come back later," I said.

"Only to come back later," Rich agreed. "We didn't know where the map was, just somewhere in the adobe and figuring we wouldn't get another chance to get in there again with the heat from both Moses and Daniel, we went back, knocking on the bricks until we found the ones that concealed the map."

Rich reached behind her and I reached for my gun. She put up her hands, showing me she held a map in one of her hands.

"That's all we wanted," she said. "The map."

"A life for a hand drawing," I said. "Pretty cheap."

"Cheap? Cheap? Nothing of the sort! Look Mike, let me show you something." Rich crouched down by the wood, metal and stone mechanical device. "See this? This is a press. A homemade press! Armando took the gold he found in the gold fields of the Sierras, smelted it down in these rocks, then poured the liquid gold into this mold and press. And see this," Rich pointed to an area of the roof of the cave that was lighter in color than the rest. "Rocks and boulders have been falling for some time now. This one on the floor, over here, knocked over this small basket, maybe decades ago, spilling the contents." She reached into the basket and pulled out a handful of gold coins. "Maybe some of these coins went over the edge, found their way into these fast moving creeks, were washed out to the coast that is only a few miles away and stayed there until your partner found one of them."

Rich was excited and talking fast. She stood up and took a step toward me but the wave of my gun stalled her steps. "And not only that," she continued talking as if unfazed, "what the gold is in is probably more valuable, rarer than the gold itself. It is a basket made by the Ohlones, and a very old one. It has to be older than Armando himself. There really aren't that many of these that survived over time. We're really lucky we found these, especially now. Look at this cave. It really is unstable. Right above our heads is a large crack above the fire pit. The rock probably got overheated and cracked and now over the years, with the heat of the summer and cold of the winter, the water, it looks as if this large slab is ready to fall."

I looked up. I could see some gaps and cracks in the ceiling. It really didn't look like a good idea to continue to hang out there.

"Come on," I said, "let's go."

Rich's face contorted and I could see anger welling up in her. "Can't you just imagine what we have here?" She yelled, "Can you just open your eyes for one moment?"

"I see it. I see everything," I said, "but it's not ours to keep. It's not yours to keep. The original owner," I motioned towards Amado, "intended to pass along his treasure to just one man. And now that they both have long since passed, it will be up to the courts to decide who now owns it."

"Are you crazy!" Rich screamed, "This belongs to us now! Finder's keepers! No fricken way I'm going to give this up! No way! No one else needs to know that we found Armando's gold!"

"Yeah, maybe we wouldn't have to let anyone else know," I said, "but that doesn't mean I can get let you get away with murder, and during the trial, it would eventually come out that we found it. Come on, let's go." I moved deeper inside the cave to allow Rich to pass in front of me and to head out first, "I'll hate to see you put away, for awhile, I actually liked you."

Rich didn't move and instead she just stared at me, with a dumbfounded look on her face.

"I see you haven't dropped or put back the gold you pulled out of that basket," I said, "and you have it all wrong, Rich." I continued, "His name wasn't Armando, it was Amado. Beloved."

Rich stared at me for a moment and when it sunk in that I wasn't going to let her get away with it, she responded by grabbing at her machete and making a motion as if she was going to try to throw it at me. My natural instincts kicked in and I fired my gun as I avoided the flying machete. Rich's body twisted from the initial impact of the bullet before straightening up. She stared at the reddening hole in her shirt, then at me with a surprised look on her face. She released her hold of the gold coins and they fell to the floor. I watched as a couple rolled out of the cave and off the cliff. Amado's partially mummified body joined me in watching as Rich turned, took a few steps, then fell through the cave's Manzanita curtain and out to the valley below.

That was when I started hearing the grinding of rock against rock. The crack in the cave roof was expanding and dust began to rain down from the ceiling of the cave. I took one last look at Amado's mummified body then took off running, heading for the ledge that led from the cave to the rope. I could hear the falling of some rocks within the cave behind me as I went, their echoing falls seemingly encouraging more rocks to fall, encouraging the ledge I was scrambling across to begin to crumble.

I moved at a frantic pace. Things were moving. There was a roar and the ground beneath my feet and cliff face began to shake and give way. I ran the fastest I've ever run in my life and jumped to the rope and grabbed hold of it just as the ledge I had been on started to fall away. The air, when the cliff gave way, seemed to try to suck me down with the falling rocks to the valley below but I held onto the rope, wrapping it around my arm. From where I dangled, I watched as a large slab of granite above the cave collapsed, with rocks, dirt and dust spewing out from the cave and cliff face.

I dangled for a few moments, awestruck as rock and dirt continued to fall and billowing clouds of dirt and dust began to well up from the valley below.

The cave was now completely sealed, gone, as were the artifacts, the gold, Amado as well as the ledge to the cave and down below, Rich Fortune, buried beneath tons of rock.

17

J OE AND I AGREED that the best and fastest way to get past what had transpired over the past couple of weeks was to get everything out into the open as soon as possible so Joe made another deal with Arthur McCoy and we gave him an exclusive. And I must admit, when he published the story, Arthur generally stuck with the facts, though I know his follow-up stories about the incidents would probably be skewed one way or another.

Arthur also covered both Daniel's and Moses' memorials. Daniel's memorial was held in front of the wooden cross on the grounds of Sanchez Adobe. Now every time I pass that place, I think about Daniel, his memorial, his love for his job and history and how he would sneak into the adobe at night and leave a light on in the upper floor as he slept the night away. Moses' memorial was held at the Moose Lodge. Poor guy. Whenever I grab a coffee at P-Town café in the little red caboose, or sing a song on a karaoke night at Moses' old haunt, Vallamar Station, I think of him and his grandpappy. Both memorials were nice, but I still couldn't shake the overall sadness I felt for the loss of both of them. I wish I knew the trick those women back at the gift shop in Mission Dolores had, so I could envision them being in a happier place.

Overall, I guess it took about two months for things to die down, the story of Amado and the gold and the deaths of those involved. And as these things began to settle down in the larger world, my sorrows over Daniel and Moses began to be replaced by a general unease growing in my own little world. It was as if a shadow of some unfinished business just out of sight was growing in the back of my mind. It took a bit to remember, with all the recent dramatic events but when I finally remembered it, it sent a chill down my spine. It was the idea of Colin's employer having interest in me, in my dealings with Laura Grandviewer and her West Coast smuggling ring and now, most assuredly, the end of his dealings with Rich and Colin.

I spoke to Joe about my concerns and he advised that I should move to a place that I would be able to make more secure, that I should change my habits and always carry a gun. I told him I never lived in fear before and wouldn't start now.

He also suggested that we should go on the offensive, to try to find out who was Colin's employer. We both did some research into Colin's past, but came up with nothing and since there really wasn't anything we could go off of besides the letter Colin had given me, it turned out all that we could really do was to sit and wait; it was up to my new friend to make another move. I saved the letter in a filing cabinet in my home office.

Having made the determination that things were currently out of my hands on that front, and with things seemingly falling into place at the Tenderloin office, as Steve and Marilyn were working well together and Ozzie was learning some basic Internet sleuthing, my mind finally began to feel at ease so I decided to make a change in my life, one that meant I would no longer sleep alone.

From my tool chest, I pulled out a screwdriver and changed my bedroom door handle back to the lever style so Poseidon could break in whenever he wanted. He seemed pleased when I closed the door the first time with the new-old handle; he immediately tested it and opened the door within a minute.

I picked Poseidon up as he strutted into my bedroom and carried him over to our now shared bedroom window. I cracked it open to let in some fresh air, turned on the radio and retrieved the glass of Jameson I had poured myself prior to working on the bedroom door handle. For the next couple of hours, I savored this time of peace as Poseidon and I listened to music, gazed into the night sky and onto Montara Mountain.

MIKE MASON'S NOTEBOOK TIMELINE

1769—The Portola Expedition, searching for Monterey Bay, unknowingly stumbles upon and views San Francisco Bay from the top of what is now Sweeny Ridge.

1776—The Declaration of Independence signed. In June of the same year, Misión San Francisco de Asís, what is later called Mission Dolores, is founded.

1785—1789 San Pablo y Asistencia, an outpost to grow food for Mission Dolores, is established along side of an Ohlone village called Pruristac. This site is also where the Sanchez Adobe will late be built.

1791—1796 Remaining villagers of Pruristac are wiped out by diseases and San Pablo y Asistencia is abandoned.

1810—1821 The Mexican War of Independence from Spain is waged. During this time, relations between California's Missions and Mexico are strained. Mission Dolores's Indian population reaches roughly 1,000 persons, yet huge numbers are continually lost to disease. In 1820, Amado arrives at Mission Dolores.

1834—The Mexican government takes over the Missions and most church property is sold or given to private owners.

1839—Don Francisco Sanchez is granted the land that basically becomes Pacifica.

1842—1846 Sanchez Adobe is built.

1848—California is ceded to the United States, gold is discovered near Sacramento, California, and Amado disappears to the gold country, along with most of San Francisco.

1858—Amado returns to San Francisco, along with Emperor Norton.

1861—1865 The American Civil War.

1871—1878 Amado attempts to purchase the adobe but is denied the opportunity and becomes a squatter until Bank of American forecloses on the property for unpaid debts.

1879—1880's Amado is noted as being seen in San Francisco when Emperor Norton passes away. The new owner of Sanchez Adobe extensively remodels the property.

1906—San Francisco Earthquake. Mission Dolores comes out relatively unscathed.

1908—Ocean Shore Railroad trains run from San Francisco to Half Moon Bay. Amado is often seen as a passenger or found hanging out at the various stations.

1920—Amado disappears with the last Coastside train. Tales of his lost gold and the possibility of there being a treasure map circulate for a time.

1947—The Sanchez Adobe is sold to San Mateo County and·a restoration of the site begins.

1957—The city of Pacifica is created by incorporating a group of connecting beach communities.

A HINT OF THINGS
TO COME . . .

BOOK III

COASTSIDE

DETECTIVES

DISTANT ISLANDS

By Matthew F. O'Malley

1

IT WAS EARLY ON a Monday morning when my ringing cell phone woke me up from a deep sleep. On the line was Tony Chin of the Pacifica Police Department, directing me to meet him out at the Mussel Rock Transfer Station Disposal Site out over on Westline Drive.

"You know what time it is?" I asked.

"Have something I want you to see," Tony replied.

"Can't see over the phone," I replied. "What time is it?"

"Six-thirty."

"Jeez!" I replied, "Call me back in a couple of hours."

"I need you to come out here, now!" Tony commanded. "Over at the transfer station. I have something I want you to see."

"Let me guess," I said. "Trash."

"Listen. I'm in no mood for jokes. I need you out here now."

"I'm in no mood for jokes, either. You just woke me up from a beautiful dream with a young healthy blonde."

"You want me to send some of the boys over to get you?"

"All right, all right," I said. "I can meet you over there in a bit."

"Half an hour?" Tony asked.

"Half an hour," I replied.

Tony's a good guy but he's very by the book and is constantly rubbing my nose in the line that separates what people in my line of work can do and what requires law enforcement. Over the years, he has made it crystal clear if anytime he catches me crossing that boundary, he will not give me any slack.

"Well, Poseidon, time to get up," I said. Poseidon, my orange tabby, had made his way into my bedroom during the night by jumping up and pulling down on the bedroom lever handle. He now stretched and yawned and looked up at me from his pillow on my bed.

I took a long, hot shower to shake my hangover, and while I was dressing, my phone rang. It was Tony. I didn't pick up. After dressing, I went downstairs, fed Poseidon and then drove down Oddstad Boulevard where I gassed up at the station at the corner of Terra Nova. I then headed over the hill to catch a scenic view of the Pacific Ocean as I drove down Fassler Avenue. My phone rang a few more times. Each time it was Tony. I was beginning to think our meeting might actually be important.

I slowly made my way out toward the Manor District of Pacifica, stopping first at the P-Town café for a cup of java. I then moseyed down Highway One, passing Sharp Park Golf Course; it looked green, The Little Brown Church looked brown, and then Sam's Castle looked gray. I really wasn't in a rush; too early in the morning, on a Monday, having a hangover, and especially when it was a request by a police officer, which meant I was about to get hassled.

I took the Manor exit off of Highway One and drove up Palmetto Ave. to Westline Drive. The roads of Palmetto and Westline are absolutely stunning, with views of the Pacific. If headed south in the opposite direction I was driving, you'd get dramatic views of the Pacific and can see the entire length of Pacifica. The north end of Westline Drive, just beyond the transfer station and the direction I was heading, ends at a nice little parking lot above the Pacific. On a clear day, you can look north and see all the way up to the Marin Headlands north of San Francisco and across the Golden Gate Bridge, or you can spend your time watching the hang gliders soar and eventually land nearby, weather permitting. People walk their dogs along the trails from the lot down to the beach or spend time just pondering the nice-sized coastal cliffs and the homes perched above them that are doomed to their eroding destruction.

I wanted to head over to that parking lot, finish my coffee and watch the ocean waves, but the phone calls from Tony kept coming. Eventually, I needed to make the appointment, so I turned off of Westline Drive and headed in.

Mussel Rock Transfer Station is just inside the Daly City limits and bordering Pacifica, so I wasn't too surprised to see a couple of Daly City police cars were parked alongside some Pacifica police cars just outside of the hump in the road that leads to the transfer station. One of the Pacifica officers recognized me and waved me in. Over the hump and through a cyclone fence gate and one is upon the transfer station grounds. Inside the grounds is a small weigh station, followed by an enormous one-sided shed with large bays where you can park your car or truck and dump your household or contractor trash. A large yellow tractor at times compresses the trash the best it can, and later dumps the compacted trash into beds of semi trucks that haul it to wherever trash goes.

On this visit, there were no paying customers dropping off trash, just a parking area full of Pacifica and Daly City police cars parked haphazardly about and a coroner's ambulance. The air was filled with squawking seagulls and putrid air and when I drove up, Tony Chin was standing by the weigh station and talking to a couple of officers. He immediately spotted me and walked toward my car. I meet him halfway.

"What took you so long?" He sounded annoyed so I jumped on it.

"Had to pretty myself up," I responded.

"For the dumps?" he asked.

"For the dumps," I replied.

"I called you a couple of times. You said it would take you half an hour. It took you an hour an a half. What took you so long, and why didn't you pick up? Did you go somewhere between your house and here?"

"Look," I said, "I had to stop and get some coffee, and you do know you're not allowed to use a phone while driving in California."

"Get a headset," Tony said.

"Those things mess with my ears. Look, what's this about?"

"Follow me," Tony said. He led me over to the trash shed, where I stopped.

Filth was absolutely oozing from the piles of garbage and out toward the entrance of the shed; I just knew my first step inside would cover the soles of my shoes in rank, raw sewage, so I opted to stay outside. Inside, I could see ripped open trash bags, doors, clothing, suitcases, decomposing food waste, and housing rubble—everything you expect to see in such a place, except for the human body partially covered and lying amid the muck. It looked as if he had a rag stuffed into his mouth.

"Do you know this man?" Tony asked.

"Nope," I said, "can't say that I do. But that's not saying much, since he is pretty busted up."

"Why don't you come a little closer?"

Upon seeing there was a dead body involved, I knew I had to go in. Immediately I felt myself sliding along the concrete floor, though I made it to the outskirts of the piles of trash without falling.

Tony snickered as he watched me make my way to him. He was standing on top of some bags of garbage and right next to the body.

"Now again I ask, do you know this man? Can you tell me anything about the situation we have here?" Tony asked, as if I knew something.

I looked closer at the man. He was wearing a red Pendleton collared shirt over a stained wife-beater. His jeans were well worn, faded and stained, looking like the stains were from before his garbage dive. He had one red scruffy Wolverine boot on with its apparent twin lying amid a pile of soiled magazines. His brown hair was curly, matted in places, and wet from the garbage sludge he was laying in. His body looked like he was fairly in shape, except for his head, which looked as if it had been bashed about with a baseball bat. And what from a distance had looked like a rag stuffed into his mouth was actually a crab, a dead ocean-floor crawling crab. It was quite sizable and stuffed halfway into the man's mouth. It actually looked like it got stuck climbing sideways out of the man's bruised orifice. "I guess you can probably rule out suicide," I finally said as I stared at the crustacean.

"You recognize him?" Tony asked.

I looked closely at the man. His face was cut and bruised in red, purple and death yellow. "Can't say that I do."

"Is that so?" Tony said. "Look closer and tell me what you see is wrong with this picture."

I leaned forward and looked at the man and looked closely at the dead crab.

"From what I can tell," I said, "it is a Dungeness crab and although it is crab season, this one is undersized so it is illegal for this man to have it on his person. Have you contacted Fish and Game?"

"Don't be a smartass!" Tony growled. "Look closer. Look at his shirt pocket."

I looked at the man's unbuttoned shirt pocket and saw what looked like a piece of paper. I used the fingernail of my index finger to pull open his pocket so I could look inside. What I found was a business card that read *Coastside Detectives*.